Do I Look Like A Lighthouse?

Granny Nanny

Contents

The Start 5
Young Me 6
Childhood 11
Children 16
Army Quarters 1 18
Army Quarters 2 21
Nativity 24
The Old Coffee Shop 29
Do I Look Like a Cow? 32
Random Thoughts 37
Casualty 42
Curly Wurly Baby 46
Freedom At Last 50
Hobbies 53
Greensleeves 57
In-Laws 60
Holidays 64
Making A Good Impression 68
Rotary 71
Chipping Sodbury (Sodding Chipbury) 76
Guest House Devon 81
Womens Institute 84
London 87
Sport 89
Team Work 91
Navigation 93
The Middle, Or Maybe Past It! 95
Mobiles 96
Television 98
Ageism 100
Names 102
Horse In A Sitting Room 104
Millennium New Year 106
The End 108

I
The Start

Do I look like a Lighthouse? Well some folks might think I do, I am oldish, (ok, old), and shall we say, of the sturdy variety of womanhood. I stand proud, often on my own, but the only time my head lights up is when I have an idea! I have had a few of those as you will read, and some better than others, but apparently I was named "The Lighthouse" by my grown-up children, who say I have steered them away from the rocks during their varied lives. Always there from a distance, but keeping a lookout for them and their families. Mmm, lets just say I try my best. At a family gathering the other day, and probably after a tiny spot of fizz, my grown up granddaughter asked if the Lighthouse analogy was because the lights are on, but there's no one at home!! Caused great hilarity I have to say, with the whole family enjoying our 55th Wedding Anniversary. Haha, think she is probably spot on ~ or rather IS spot on! I admit it!

I have actually seen many, many lighthouses during my roaming life, but never wanted to go into one. Think I may be claustrophobic in there, but perhaps it's the lack of lifts, I don't know, but the thought of all those stairs..! Bad enough climbing the stairs to my bedroom in my son's house! 2 long floors up (to retrieve a mobile I had forgotten) is etched in my brain ~ I have investigated where a lift might be fitted in there, but he's not having any of it.

So here I am, contemplating and watching my own family grow into such diverse but wonderful humans, and lucky for me, I also watch as their own families do the same. I like it when they laugh at me after a Prosecco (or two), whoop-whooping as I say the wrong thing to the wrong people, they love that one!

I also realise that I have not always been this old, and have had the happiest of lives whilst the memory was still intact, which was the reason I thought to write things down. I am guessing that when I am REALLY off my mind, I can read about it, and will think it's someone else's story! Well that's the theory anyway, and I know for sure my grown up grand daughter will happily inform me when I do!

The following then, is a snapshot of life seen through the bottom of a Gin and Tonic or two, but mixed up in time ~ due to age, and memory loss. (Funny how I always remember to plant the mint ready for a Summer Pimms though)..... Selective, this loss of memory!

II
Young Me

My goodness!! I visited a museum, and what do you think? I found a school classroom, complete with all the paraphernalia of a 1950s schoolroom, and couldn't for the life of me work out why other visitors were in awe of what looked like to them, a symbol of medieval learning. As for me ~ I felt truly at home in those surroundings, with the map of the world on the wall, the teachers high desk, where she would perch on her high chair, and what looked like Victorian ipads, but which I knew were slate boards!! To write on with chalk!! And felt rubbers, to rub out the chalk!!

The wooden desks in rows all facing the front, with ink wells that needed filling with ink by the ink monitor, and I can tell you that I rose to that dizzy height of ink monitor!! Well,~ not for very long, cause when I filled one particular ink well, (using a very heavy LARGE bottle of ink), I overdid the trickle, and the ink cascaded into the desk, turning one poor girl's shiny white gleaming tennis kit blue/black!!!

Think my long-time friend Ellen would sympathise, relatively recently, I sat at her lunch table with a glass of red wine and just as her husband told a funny story, and just as I was about to take a drink, I laughed, and splattered deep red splatters all over her shiny white gleaming table-cloth. Do you see a pattern emerging?

Sorry, I have rambled away from the museum, but actually nothing more to be said, except to keep my mouth tightly shut in a museum in the future, my grandchildren quite, quite embarrassed by Grandma actually living in that by-gone era. Must avoid the other museum in York, the one with Roman artefacts, and come to think of it, the dinosaur exhibits. They already call me T Rex due to my having what they think to be short arms, cause I am unable to reach the top shelves in the kitchen!! (I THINK that's why they call me T Rex - I could be wrong!!

The young me, was born in Bolton (someone has to be), and the story goes that my mother and the above mentioned Ellen's mother were giving birth a few days apart, in the same Maternity ward. Found they lived just around the corner from each other, and so the 2 girls became friends. We grew up together, played together, and went on holidays together ~ and, more or less, were both the same person.

She was there when I cut off one of my plaits whilst on holiday on Anglesey, and on some days, I had to share her with my younger sister, which I DID NOT LIKE!! When we were having one sweaty run-around at my house, her mother uttered the immortal lines, "Ellen, stop sweating!!" Classic! We played Cluedo on Sundays, which led us on the detective trail, which, if your young girls were to do this today, would horrify you. We followed men!! Boys or men, we didn't care, but we made a check-list of clothing to look out for, and various types of men to pursue, and in our leather bound books which I made, we listed where they were going and who they met. We followed them if they fitted our criteria, then went to the phone boxes (to ring HQ), pressing button B if someone answered! Or was it button A? No, it was B to get your money back! Or was it the other way round? Parents not happy ~ you can never please them can you?

For some very strange reason, my mother wouldn't let me wear short white socks until June!!! Instead, I had to persevere with thick, knee length ones, usually beige, the worst ones being grey!! Dark Grey!! And clumpy, lace-ups!! How I longed for the white socks and sandals that Ellen wore in April and May, but no, I had to wait in the sticky heat which comes with running around in the sunshine. "Never cast a Clout till May is out" was my mother's mantra, and as usual, no use arguing. So, sweaty, and clumpy was how I spent my April and May ~ oh, and miserable too!! Roll on Anglesey in June then, when I could kick them off and enjoy the freedom!

Ellen and I grew into teenagers, went to cinemas, and clubs and Bolton Palais, and eventually I was her bridesmaid at her wedding. I looked forward to her being mine, a year later, but she was pregnant, and well, you can't have a pregnant bridesmaid on the photos can you!!!

Have I rambled again? My mind flitting back to the day when I started at Primary School, and I was just 5. Don't think I remember THAT much about it, except on that first day I just walked home at play-time! Thought the school day was over, so I legged it. Teacher came to the house, and my dad promised I would go back to school the day after, if I could stay at home that day. It worked, and I never bothered to play truant again!! LOVED Primary, but Secondary School I hated. All girls, and bitchy, and except for English and History, nothing excited me. One English teacher, Mrs King, used to sit on a stool facing us, with legs crossed, and her finger firmly up her nose, picking away at heaven knows what, and wiping the offending haul onto her long knicker leg!! Wonder why I wasn't impressed?

My Needlework teacher was lusting after my Sports teacher, who I hated with a passion ~ it was she who made me stand in line to be picked for teams, and no one wanted me 'cause I hated sport, and sweaty things, but the humiliation of being "last one standing" stays with me to this day. The swimming was the very worst, I hated having to change communally, and as I wore a liberty bodice which had a deal of rubber surrounding it, I took my talc to help with pulling it onto my damp torso. For anyone not having come across one of these contraptions before, I can assure you they are worse than a corset!! They grab you with their rubber strips, and squeeze you tightly, so eating an extra biscuit is obviously out of the question, and I could never figure out why on earth I was made to wear one. Perhaps it was to keep me warm, and by golly it succeeded ~ only problem was ~ it cut off the circulation at the same time. Oooh, how they grabbed you!! And how hard they were to put on and take off!! Everyone laughed at the talc, and so I always feigned cramp, or an ear ache, or stomach ache, and the Nazi ~ sorry ~ swimming teacher would let me get out of that horrid deep water, which I just knew SOMEONE had been weeing in!! Result!! Could get dressed in peace, and who cared if I ever swam or not? Not me!!

Now, with a grown son and daughter-in-law who both came out of University as sports teachers, and a 25 year old granddaughter who has done the same, I wonder where on earth I went wrong!! Could be worse I suppose, they could be sitting on stools, picking their noses and teaching English!!

I never mastered riding a bike either. I had a trike, with a boot at the back for carrying my baby (ok ~ a doll), and I did quite like giving up a little of my reading time to pedal away, but the wind messing up my hair, had me running back to Enid Blyton and the Famous Five. I never wanted a two-wheeler like my sister, at least not after seeing her come home all dishevelled and wind swept. No, books were my thing!

You wouldn't think then, that I would go on a Youth Hostelling trip with my class mates, to the Lake District! But I did. And hated it. Clunky boots, tramping over moors, climbing over fells, rain in my face, and arriving back at another youth hostel wet through, and just in time to make up the bunk beds!! And peel potatoes. Not for me.

So I suppose my school didn't cater for a girl like me, there were no trips to the theatre, no outings to art galleries, and no creative writing classes. Might as well have stayed at home, which according to my school report I did, due to illness of one sort or another. I think I learned all I needed to as soon as I left that school, and continue to in my ripe old age. I feel for those children at school who are unhappy, but better things will come, there is just no rush. Instead, I had my Auntie, who took me to the ballet, to classical concerts and the theatre, who was interested in what I read, and when I told her I couldn't believe in a God, instead of tut-tutting, agreed with me. She was a true beacon, guiding me through my teenage years, and I have a lot to thank her for. Auntie Connie, I miss you!

After all, I turned out to be a sociable creature, pursued my own way in life, I hope I was a good mother, and fingers crossed I am an ok Grandma, and my husband seems to like me, so fingers up to those teachers who didn't inspire me. I never (so far) needed to swim, and heaven forbid I should attempt to ride a two-wheeler, or the traffic problem in York will be infinitely worse!!!

So I seem to have survived the Young Me, have survived the Middle Aged Me, and is there anyone who has survived the Old Aged Them? The jury is still out! (but I will try my hardest!), and if ever those liberty bodices come back into fashion, run for the hills girls!!!

III
Childhood

I led a very sheltered life. Well, that is to say, MY life was sheltered, I can't say that of my sister, who for the most part was a particular pain in the you-know-what, especially for our parents. They were hard-working newsagents who had to be up at an ugly hour (4.30am) to take delivery of the daily papers, prior to the paper-boys having their papers allocated in the correct order, ready for their rounds. The shop closed at 6pm, so a long day for them, and I suppose they really wanted a stress-free home-life, and in the most part I gave it to them. (Unintentionally).

Addicted to reading from a very early age, I was always on the settee, in front of the fire, reading whatever I could lay my hands on, usually Enid Blyton, or What Katy Did, and then What Katy did Next. I got on to Cherry Ames "nursie" books, which highlighted my very great need to become a nurse~well~ matron, to be honest! (Think I liked the uniform). I only ever met one other woman who read these books as a youngster, and SHE became a nurse in Queen Alexandra's Nursing Corps, which incidentally had the most gorgeous fluted headwear!!! Anyway, there I was, engrossed in lovely books, whilst my younger sister got on with what SHE enjoyed doing, which was to be as naughty as possible!!

Useless trying to disguise her name in this story, cause everyone in the family know who I mean. The name "SUSAAAN"!!!!! rang through the house every single day ~ her school reports telling us that the whole school could hear her, well before they saw her. The same reports that were always found in hiding places around the house several weeks after being issued.

So there we were, sisters as far apart in personality as you can find, me quite angelic (!) and Susan running the Tortoise Club!

Now, this club is probably not what you may have thought it was. My 8 year old sister talked a boy her age into showing off his dangly bits. To the girls. Probably called the Tortoise Club due to the dangly bits protruding from the encrusted underpants, and looking like a tortoise emerging from hibernation! She organised the showing, (the only stipulation being ~ no touching!) along-side our grandmas house, behind a hedge, so they couldn't be seen (not altogether daft then!) and the girls queued up to see this delight as often as they could afford to. Yes!! She charged them!! It was 2d (old money~we are very old), and the two entrepreneurs pocketed 1d each. Seems that everyone was a winner then, and believe me, the queue snaked right down the avenue, so they were quids- in. I joined the queue once, then got scared and ran away, so sister charged me anyway, and I was scared to tell! (I run away from tortoises to this day)

Don't know for sure if this was after the painting incident or before it, but I don't know what went through her mind when she painted the bathroom. She was SO angry that our parents didn't appreciate her hard work, but to give them their due, their white, white faces matched their white, white rage, and they were unable to do anything with that rage, the sight before them, stopping all coherent thought processes. The inside of the bath was daubed in baby pink gloss, the taps in blue. The middle panels of the doors in the pink, the rest blue. What should have been a toilet roll, was disguised with paint, to blend in with the toilet roll stand which was a mixture of the two colours. Quite artistic, and a look that Tracey Emin would have been proud of ~ pity my mother couldn't see the potential, but there you are, you can never do your best for a parent can you? Sister had started to paint the floor tiles, but ran out of paint, and there she stood, with the brush still in her hand whilst the now almost-in-a-faint mother let out an almighty howl that would have impressed that Werewolf in London! Bit over the top, these mothers they like a good show of misery! And I have to say, there was a VERY good show of misery during the next week or two. And tears. Oh Lord, lots of those, probably enough to fill the wretched pinkish-in-places bath!!

We lived in a house that was at the back of our shop, and the side wall of the house ran along the side street, off the main road, but see-able from a way off. My fathers short step ladders were somewhere near the side door, and my angelic sister thought the wall was a tad on the plain side, and in another Tracey Emin moment, thought to add something to it's blandness. She found some chalk, and from the top of the ladder wrote on the wall **** OFF (I am repressed, and unable to write that word, let alone say it!) in large letters. Now. I have no idea if she knew what that meant, I am supposing one of the paper boys had thought to educate her, but I can't be sure. Someone informed my dad of the art work looming large at the side of the house, and he quickly gave her a telling off, along with a bucket and scrubbing brush. Whilst he was in the shop again, she did what he had asked, but unfortunately scrubbed in the very direction of the offending letters, leaving the same letters visible, but this time as clean letters, not chalk ones. Uh oh! More misery!!

Then there was Lou!!!! Our great-aunt was a member of the Amateur Dramatic Club, and gave us "Lou" which was an old ventriloquist doll, the head being made from papier mache, and the body ~ well ~ just a floppy piece of random cloth with papier mache hands. So far, it doesn't sound too bad does it, except to me, it was the scariest thing I had ever seen (hadn't seen the tortoise though, come to think of it!).

The head was long and narrow, and was once white. There was a painted black hairline at the front, LARGE black and red staring eyes, and a huge red mouth that opened wide to reveal pointed teeth when the string in its inside was pulled. The mouth made a horrid rasping hiss when opened, but worst of all ~ worst of all ~ was the long nose. It must have been about 9 inches long, and was red at the end. This nose was used by my sister to hold onto as she chased me around the house with it, and chase me she did!! ALL the time, and I screamed ALL the time! It was hideous. I hated it, and I hated her, especially when she put it in my bed, and as I threw the bedding back to get in, there was Lou leering at me, looking at me, and planning evil to me. I have the same fear when I see clowns, not fear of them really, but fear of Lou ~ who KNOWS where he may be lurking. I hope he is dead, and buried under tons of horse manure and full non disposable nappies!! And concrete!

As a teenager she got a pen pal called Hugh Frew, a "teddy boy" from Glasgow, who turned out to be non-too-sharp, but who wanted to visit with his teddy-boy friends. Mother said no! She was getting quite used to that word by now, but was still using up the hankies at an alarming rate!

Funnily enough, Sue grew up~ well ~ got older, and continued to plague ME instead of our parents, letting my children do anything they liked when she was with them. Stuffing Easter Eggs into them before breakfast, even before WE were up, and causing our eldest to throw up sitting in front of his corn flakes, after 3 chocolate eggs. Letting him unroll toilet rolls because it was fun, letting them all watch inappropriate films when they stayed with her, including The Exorcist!!!   Good Lord ~ I even banned Grange Hill in our house, ~
everyone knows it was the sole reason for bad behaviour in our schools up and down the country!

Anything my children wanted, she got for them, including

the most horrendous of dresses for our daughter, who had a smile all over her face when she saw me with the tears and hankies myself! She became known as Titty Sue, because our daughter couldn't say Auntie ~ and still is I have to say!! (Titty Sue, that is!!).

She did manage to find employment, or at least blackmailed the boss to get it, and became assistant factory manager of a clothing firm making raincoats for Marks and Spencer, who were very very picky picky, and who inspected the clothing with a magnifying glass, and some of the clothes she knew, were not up to M&S standards. On the inspection days, she had the staff load the dross onto a lorry, and had it drive around Manchester for the day, until the inspectors had gone!!

Still causing bother ~ but now she is retired, and relatively calm, we can all rest easy and know that we survived!!

You will see that I am squeaky clean through all this (!) the only naughty thing I ever did was to cut off one of my plaits, whilst on holiday. Got fed up with plaits, and used my mother's nail scissors to get rid, but only managed to cut one off, before I heard my mother coming upstairs, Had the plait in my hand still with the satin bow attached, and as the footsteps got nearer, hid it behind the dressing table!! The only "punishment" being a trip to the hairdresser, which to me was a great outcome, and for her, her eldest cutting off a plait was a tiddler compared to the antics of her youngest!! And not a tear in sight!

As for now, my dearest sister lives on one side of the Pennines, and me on the other. Up to the reader to speculate on which is the better side of course, but don't you just love that word, Karma?

IV
Children

I've never been that keen on babies really, even mine raised my stress levels to dangerous proportions, ~ with teething, sleepless nights, and my endless search for a bit of peace and quiet. That last bit was like hunting for a dress that makes you look a size 6!! Never to be found!

Toddlers with their tantrums and their fussy eating take some looking after, and again THE SEARCH. This time the search for a lone bath or shower, when even a trip to the toilet (alone) was a celebration in itself. Other mothers in the same boat, so what do we do? We meet up for a coffee ~"Oh how lovely, let's do it every week!", we say at the start of the great toddler trek through life. But what is that looked-forward-to-coffee-get-together like? Sometimes hell, that's what it's like!!! Talking to a friend, toddler gets up close, and turns your face away from the friend, to look at THEM. You may think you are grown up enough to deal with this scenario, but you end up like putty in their tiny hands, frantically trying to make eye-contact with the friend, whilst struggling with a toddlers iron grip! It's surprising how many books a toddler can pull off a bookshop shelf whilst you are pouring milk into that cup of coffee! Waterstones ~ I apologise!!

The tantrums are for mothers who cannot control their children, (said you, when you were pregnant), but here you are in the throes of another screaming fit because you gave your tot a blue cup, and not the orange one!!! Smiling at the crowd gathering to gawp is useless, trying to grab an arm is useless, ~ and with the sweat beginning to roll down the back of the neck at this stage and calling them "darling" as they are rammed into their pushchair does nothing for the blood pressure!

But then, they get bigger! They begin to talk, and how I love it when they can chatter all day, ~ and make me laugh ~ and give hugs and kisses without a tear in sight. Lovely. I saw a programme on television before Christmas, where 5 year olds were taken to a residential home, where the residents were sceptical about this funny mix of ages, but the sheer exuberance of the children rubbed off on the elderly, and they all got stuck into games, and card-making, with glitter all over the place. Happy children. Happy residents. And friendships continuing.

I might be one in a million, but loved when mine were teenagers!! Yes I did, they were fun, I liked most of their friends, they included me in the things they were interested in (well~ to a point), and to see them mature into what they are now, made all the tantrums worthwhile! Am beginning to sound a bit self-satisfied I know, but I am sitting here and missing them!!

All 3 have their own families, all 3 still like to "come home", no matter where that might be, and they have all supported me through MY tantrums, as I get older!! AND I know who to turn to for help with IT, when my husband has given up on my learning to copy and paste!

Not everyone has that ability to rely on someone else when things go pear-shaped, and that is precisely why, when I retired, I volunteered as an Advocate for older people. Many problems can be solved easier with someone else to discuss it with, and for that someone to actually do your writing, or telephoning, or whatever it is that needs a helping someone to solve it with you. Ok then, I could never solve how to copy and paste for anyone, including myself, bit I sure do know who to ask for help! My daughter ~ the one with the blue cup, instead of the orange one!

V
Army Quarters 1

I don't know if it is the same now, but when my husband was in the Army, and I followed him from country to country, we were allocated "Quarters" according to our husband's rank. Never mind if a Colonel and his wife, who had no children, would be happy with a 2 bedroom flat -----NO----- they had to have the requisite 4 bedroom detached with study and an extra cooker. (not in the study by the way). Captains got a 3 bed semi, Majors got a 4 bed detached, and Colonels the same but with the said study and said extra cooker. By the time your husband made it to General, you had your drive cleared of snow!! Not as simple as it sounds, 'cause a soldier had to come out first thing in the morning to measure the snow, and if it was over 1 inch deep, it got cleared. Same with leaves in the Autumn. Which reminds me of a parade in Germany, during a windy Autumn.

Leaves festooned the parade ground the day before the important parade, and still lots of leaves clung to the branches for dear life. It was decided to deploy a helicopter (!) to hover over the trees in order to relieve the branches of their stoic leaves, followed by a leaf vacuum to suck up the offending debris. No one wanted the visiting General to have to cast his critical eye on even one orange, curled up, wayward leaf. He was surely going to be impressed.

I, personally, thought he WAS impressed, however, as the soldiers stood to attention on the exquisite parade ground, with the majority of the Regiment's 1000-strong soldiers on parade, a hush descended as he was about to arrive. My husband, as second in command was standing right at the front, with sword poised, seemingly ready for an invasion!! The assembled on-lookers were seated, and silenced... mainly proud wives and their children, and the air of calm anticipation was almost palpable.

His car arrived, and the Colonel of the Regiment escorted him past the silenced on-lookers. I was on the front row of the seats with my 8 year old daughter, and we sat alongside the Colonel's wife and her daughter, also 8. Now! My daughter has always had a rather piercing voice, and with her index finger firmly pointing at the Colonel as he passed, she shouted, "Hey, I've seen his willy!!" I can't really explain the feelings I had during the next few seconds. I noticed a tightening of the buttocks of the 2 men passing by us, and a slight twitch on the eye of the Colonel, indicating to me that he had indeed heard! I thought I heard 'Social Services' whispered somewhere behind me, but I could have been mistaken.

It is here I believe I should explain to you what had happened the night before. My daughter had had a sleepover at her friends house..(yes, the Colonel's daughter), and her father had gone to the loo during the night, (naked) quite forgetting about the sleepover. Well, enough said, except there was a rush on pyjamas in the NAAFI for the next few days!!.

Oh I always ramble and I forgot that I started to tell you quite a different story: one about Quarters. I shall focus.

We arrived in Germany with 2 small children and were in the process of being "marched-in" to our new home, a 3 bed semi. You can deduce from that, that my husband was indeed a Captain. "Marching-in" and "Marching-out" had become a stressful part of our lives. Taking over the house, having contents checked with inventory etc, and accompanied by the endless search for dirt! Any dirt found, and any dirty marks on walls and doors have to be paid for by the out-going occupant, and so it pays to inspect thoroughly. When leaving a quarter, and ahead of the "march-out", we would remove any sign that we had lived in the house, scrubbing and polishing the oven to within an inch of its life. "They", the men employed to inspect, would kneel down and inspect the oven using a torch to highlight any skulking splashes of food, and finding a crumb would send them tut-tutting for their invoice pad. A mark on the wall or door would be DM 1, and so it went upwards. Oh dear, I digress.

Here we were, standing in our new home, and looking at the cooker hob with only 3 rings instead of the 4 we were used to. The 4th had never been there, and in its favour, left room for a spoon rest or some-such. That was the only plus. I stared at it for some time, and "they" didn't seem to notice, or care, or both. On they went with their counting. I had to say something. "Excuse me", I said "but why are there only 3 rings on the hob?" Total disbelief from "them". Eyebrows raised, they stared at me, unblinking, unflinching, just chilling disbelief. He opened his pursed lips and asked what my husband's rank was. Captain. "Well" he said, "If you want 4 rings you had better get him promoted to Major". Now it was my turn for the disbelief bit. I was lost for words....well, for about a minute!

Rambling again I know, sorry, but whilst we are on the subject...... that house was quite clean except for the cooker and fridge. The out-goers had been charged DM75 and a slap on the wrist and again, I had to ask a question. (which they weren't used to!) "Are you going to clean the cooker and fridge as the out-goers had paid to have it cleaned by "them"?" Reasonable question I thought, but no, "they" were not having any of it. I came up with a cunning plan. "Well I will willingly clean them myself, and you can give me the DM75". He was getting mad. "You can clean them, but you won't get any money."

I did clean them, and got them very clean indeed, and the morning after, I went with my 2 children to collect my money. The Estate Office was full of "thems", and I went to the desk of my "them", and asked very politely for my DM75. A hush fell upon the room, followed by shuffling of chairs, and with my "them" waving his arms he escorted me off the premises. I went... but I returned the following morning. Same thing. I went every morning for the next 6 weeks, and oh my! Was he annoyed! A controlled annoyance you understand.... an annoyance where he would rather punch the filing cabinet but had to keep himself in check. An annoyance where you can see he is weighing up whether he really needs this job, or whether he can explode and say what he really wants to say.

Eventually something wonderful happened. After 6 weeks of persecution he opened the drawer of the filing cabinet, and very slowly took DM75 out of the petty cash box. He passed it to me, very carefully, his face red and blotchy, and put it on the desk in front of me. I took it, folded it, and said, "Thank you SO much, this is so good of you". Off I went to spend my money on a new skirt and jumper. How satisfied was I? There are no words!!

VI
Army Quarters 2

I think this may be the last of the Army Quarters stories. Well ~ don't celebrate ~ you just never know.

Am thinking of the time we left Malta, and our lovely posting in the Mediterranean. It was January time when we got our posting order, and we hoped we were going back to UK, but only in as much as we had our fingers crossed. Our second son had been born in Malta and we were looking forward to friends and family meeting him, along with our first born who was now a 4 year old ~ going on 24! Both boys blonde, good fun, and growing fast.

Fingers crossed then, and the letter arrived. UK!! Phew!!

Then we read on, Birmingham!! (from Malta?) then, John to be Adjutant for the TA!! AND we were going to live in a flat! It had all looked so good, and now, Oh Lord!

The 3 months of packing and cleaning our quarter to within an inch of it's life began. Our lovely friends gave us great farewell parties ~ they must have been glad to see the back of us because they did the farewelling in great style, even arriving at the airport with more champagne as we waited to board our flight home. Oh well, we thought, perhaps Birmingham won't be so bad after all, and we mopped our many, many tears away, and waved with our hankies as the plane taxied down the runway.

We arrived at our new Army- Quarter-4-bed-flat at the same time as the lorry delivering our well-packed boxes containing all our worldly goods. Gloom. The building looked awful. And it was on the 1st floor. And it was June, and drizzling. We couldn't see the sea, and we had no friends or family around us. Not for miles.

Some weeks earlier the IRA had blown up the Rotunda building in the city centre, and anti establishment graffiti was commonly sprayed all over the walls close to the Army Barracks where my husband was going to work.

Along strolled "them", the people who march you into your new home, and who complete the paper-work. And, incidentally, who charge the out-goer for dirty marks and the offending grease that might be lurking in the back of the oven. I carried our 1 year old and took the hand of my 4 year old and in we went to our psychedelic new quarter. Even as I write, I am finding it hard to to comprehend, that "they" were expecting us to roll over, and live in it! On that drizzly June day, my mood was not as it usually was!! The men in the flat at the time, including my husband, did not seem to care, nor did they notice the tears beginning to well in my eyes.

The walls of all 4 bedrooms, bathroom, sitting room, dining room and kitchen were painted in a blackberry yogurt colour. All of them. And all in gloss paint (!) Old gloss paint. The woodwork on doors and skirting boards were painted black, with lots of other colours showing through the (many) knocks that had occurred over the last few years. The curtains were gold brocade (yes, all of them), with small red pelmets, but the whole effect was skilfully brought together with the addition of the carpets. They were a bright orange, and complemented by charming large grey squirls ~ wall to wall!!

I had to use a face cloth to wipe down the bed in order to change my 1 year old's nappy (it was all I had in my suitcase), and as it was so dim, I switched on the light and saw the cobwebs festooned with abandon over the ceilings.

The "them" left, and with our boxes now piled high everywhere, (I swear they still smelled of the Mediterranean), my husband looked me in the eye, and shattered what hopes I still had left for a normal life in Birmingham. "I am going away for a few days" he said. "For 4 weeks" Now ~ I loved my husband dearly ~ or had done until this moment! He was going away to shoot at Bisley (he is a good pistol and rifle shot), and as his profession required him to be an effective killer, he could justify leaving me and his 2 children in this... well...hell hole. I could not!!

Bless my mother and auntie. They came to stay just as he left, and we set about scrubbing and cleaning. And thanks to the powers-that-be, the decorators came and blitzed the flat with paint of my choosing. From end to end. Have you tried keeping 2 lively boys away from every door awash with white gloss paint? I didn't manage it! Next came the new curtains, followed by a new suite, and last but not least the new fitted carpets. All of my own choosing. Joy of Joys.

The carpet fitters were piling the detritus of cut-offs into their van when another van arrived and the door bell rang.

The engineers had arrived ~ "We have come to fit the central heating" they said, "we will have to drill into the skirting boards and take some carpets up. Don't worry, it will only take a day or two".

It took a week. But the flat was lovely, my husband (the Corps Rifle and Pistol Champion) was back with a slipped disc, and we came to love living in Birmingham. So much so that when we were due to move, we applied to stay for another 2 years!! Our daughter was born, my husband promoted to Major, I passed my UK driving test, could negotiate Spaghetti Junction without a hitch and this family of 5 were happy with city living. Oh, and we were sorry to leave, and shed a few more tears as we headed north to Catterick!!

VII
Nativity

It's that time of year again!! Yep, invitations arrived to attend two more Nativity Plays.

Now, I have sat through endless nativities, what with 3 children, and a host of grandchildren, and although most have made me laugh out loud, they have all brought a different tear to my eye as I drive away. This year's will be no different I fear, so I will be armed with the pack of tissues, and a strong backbone along with a will of iron to congratulate them on their efforts. All the efforts tucked away as usual in the memory box, and to be remembered again after a few glasses of fizz at future get-togethers. Love it!

I haven't had any fizz just now, but once I started this, the horrors came flooding back. Think the first I attended was to see my eldest son at age 5, dressed as a shepherd in nothing but a sheepskin rug and his underpants! No shoes. The procession of similar shepherds and their sheep made their way from the back of the hall, through to the stage, where baby Jesus was waiting in his Barbie 4 poster bed. Everything was very quiet and expectant, and as my son stepped onto the stage steps, he stubbed his toe, and in a VERY loud voice said, "Bl***y Hell!!!" Every pair of eyes turned to glower at me. Tears rose.

He grew up ~ well ~ got bigger, and as an 11 year old was a roving reporter in Bethlehem, in a suit and trilby, and with PRESS on a ticket on the hat. He careered over the stage like paparazzi with his camera at the ready and shouting SCOOP SCOOP!! Mary cried!

My other son was made a King, but unfortunately had no idea where he was, or what he was supposed to do, and burst into tears when he saw me! My blonde daughter being blonde was cast as an angel, the fact she was blonde being the only stipulation for being cast as angelic! During the whole performance she constantly smacked the hands of other angels if they didn't keep to the correct script,~ whilst singing louder than anyone else, and looking daggers at the host of tinselled and winged messengers from the heavens. She has always been bossy!! Angel Gabriel cried!

Oh dear, I thought by the time my grandchildren joined the nativity cast, things would be better organised, but I fear I was wrong. My 5 year old little darling lifted his handmade donkey mask to pick his nose!! For a very long time! His cousin, at a different nursery laughed rather too loudly when a tiny little girl came to dance around the Christmas tree. She was the Christmas angel for the top of the tree, and danced her heart out, round and round the tree until she got dizzy and lurched all over the stage in what was a breath-taking display of trying to keep upright! And failing!! I stifled the laughs until I cried!!

The bossy angels' sons have not been without blame either ~ her eldest being cast as a wall (?) with withering looks at Joseph, who he really wanted to be, the year after being a Nazarene in "Call the Midwife". His brother bored to tears, and sitting on the floor almost under the corner of the stage, ~ trying but failing to push the corner of that stage up his nose!! His giant shiny gold star always getting in the way! My eyes filled up, possibly due to what could have happened had he succeeded!!!

Last years though was truly hilarious, sitting directly in front of the Inn, we had a superb view of the cardboard Inn frontage, which I think was supposed to be held up by the suitably clad Inn Keepers behind it. (A motley crew, wearing old and faded tea-towels, and perhaps too disinterested to keep a hold of the cardboard for too long!) It fell down! Time and again it fell down. As Joseph insisted on knocking at each of the three doors, it fell down again and again!! It fell down as the Inn Keepers nudged each other, and again, it ended up on the floor when they insisted on doing the script justice by shouting "THERE'S NO ROOM" in loud, exasperated voices!!!! They had had enough at this stage, and there was a lot of scowling going on!! Mary took to telling the Inn Keepers off, just like my angel daughter would have, and as she tugged at Joseph's robes to move on, the thing collapsed for the last time, even the three kings had to walk over it to get to baby Jesus! Oh my, by this stage, we were all stuffing tissues in our mouths, and the ride home was indeed a tearful journey!! But a happy one!! With happy tears!! And relief ~ relief that I wasn't an Inn Keeper's Grandma!!

And so I have my invites to this years' stunning performances, and I really can't wait!! Am taking time away from being an advocate, and revelling in my family and their efforts once again! (My 6 year old grandson already searching for a flat cap and a gilet!) Watch this space ~ It might get messy!! And tearful!!

Well, here I am again, after doing my grandma duties ~ attending the latest Carol Concert and Nativity Play. I finished the visiting of my clients beforehand, and made sure all was well for their respective Christmas's before rushing headlong into the thrill of the end of term performances! Different sorts of tears this year I have to say, from different performances, but now I feel ready for Christmas, thanks to the antics of school children and their enormous efforts to entertain!

I was feeling rather blasé about the Carol Concert my 10 year old grandson was in, thinking, well, this won't be the same without the misbehaving angels, and the baby Jesus in a Barbie 4-poster, but how surprised I was!! It was lovely! I embarrassed myself somewhat, as I sat there, with someone else's toddler squealing in my ear as the music started,~ then WHAM!! I burst into tears as the younger ones began with Rudolph the Red Nosed Reindeer!! Where did THOSE tears come from?? I have no idea!! I sat up straight, determined not to be so silly, and the rest of the performance went to plan. No music to most of the traditional carols, they were related as poems, which I thought was lovely. Ever so slowly I saw the children's eyes wandering towards the back of the room, my grandson seemingly transfixed on the back wall. Wasn't until I stood up to leave, that I spotted the large screen on that back wall, ~ complete with the words rolling up!!!

Today was the 6 year old shepherd's turn to shine in his (more or less normal) Nativity play. He wore his brothers Nazareen outfit from Call the Midwife nativity a couple of years back, which was a tad too large I admit. The bright red tea towel on his head was a stroke of genius though,~ it meant we could spot him from a distance!

This year's was titled "Straw and Order," with many cows, donkeys, angels (behaving) sheep, and of course shepherds. Only 3 of them. Oh, and there was a court judge, a gavel, and a policeman. Sorry, 2 policemen. Mary and Joseph were there but no baby Jesus. I almost forgot the army of Roman Soldiers, they made a great noise marching in their bare feet, and looked spectacular.

The policeman took his job very seriously, complete with high-vis jacket, and a truncheon. I've never seen a policeman in a nativity play before, but there's a first for everything. When he was feeling a bit bored, he tried to balance his truncheon in his shoe, which he had taken off, but still kept his serious face on!! It fell over many times, and rolled into the star sitting in front of him, who was non too pleased ~ meaning she had to retrieve it for him. As she turned to do this for the umpteenth time, her face came out of the hole in the front of the star, and where she had once looked star-like, she now looked like thunder on a really dark night!! My shepherd was seemingly very up-to-date, as he had a mobile phone to use for passing messages, which he did, with aplomb. The message was telling the other shepherds that no selfie-sticks were to be used!! PROUD GRANDMA MOMENT!!

My tears of laughter came with the boy who was the gavel for the judge!! Oh my!! For a while he was on the front row, and I have to say, he had the most expressive face!! He threw himself into those expressions with a passion, out-shining any actor playing King Lear in Stratford!!! All very well, but I believe he might have needed the toilet ~ either that or he was finding comfort in fondling his ~ shall we say ~ dangly bit!!!!! I tried to stifle the laughing, but I am well known for not being able to! The "fondling" went on far too long, and by the time the judge had decided the fate of ~ well not quite sure of who ~ the gavel's eyes had rolled too far towards the back of his head for me to continue to watch, and unfortunately I became the centre of attention when the tissue stuffed into my mouth became dislodged ~ leaving me to fumble on the floor in an effort to cover up my laughter! Roll on next year!!!

So there you have it, my Christmas feeling well and truly started, just need to meet the grandchildren and tell them how great their performances were. I wonder how the Granny of the gavel is feeling right now?

VIII
The Old Coffee Shop

If you work for Social Services there isn't much happening (visit-wise) between Christmas and New Year. At least not in the Older Persons Unit, where I worked, and after a busy-busy lead-up to Yuletide, followed by a busy-busy family Christmas, a couple of days to chill out and get rid of the paper-work build up was not that onerous. I almost looked forward to it ~ as long as I could partake of the odd mince pie. Don't you just love Boxing Day though, when you come downstairs and have a box of chocolates for breakfast? Having done that then, followed by champagne truffles for lunch, my scales were telling me to calm down and go back to work!

Don't know if you know Knaresborough or not, but take it from me there is nothing much happening there either, and when my husband suggested taking me for lunch on my first day back, I jumped at the chance. How unusual! Out for lunch ~ and on a working day? ~ MY husband??

Where to go then when most of this small market town is asleep? The only eating-place open was The Old Coffee Shop, a small tea-shop-type eatery tucked away in a tiny street off the main road.

In we stepped then, both of us in a good mood, and in expectation of a good meal, with no rush. My boss had told me to take as long as I wanted (he was nearing retirement, and was brimming with bonhomie). He had been seen sleeping during one of his own team meetings, and had woken with a start to the sound of "Oi, David!" Now retired, I know how he must have felt!

Back to lunch. The clanky bell announced our arrival at the coffee shop, and with no-one to welcome us, we chose a table, and sat down. Not a soul in the place ~ the whole of Knaresborough obviously sleeping off Christmas, ready for round 2 at New Year. My husband, always picky, saw his cup was dirty, so went round to the other tables, collecting cleaner crockery and cutlery to mix and match with ours. Satisfied, he sat down. I say satisfied, but what I really mean is DIS satisfied judging by the grumbling emanating from his very tight lips! DIRTY CUPS!!!!

Squirming in his seat (probably wondering if he dare trust the food), we met the owner, with a menu in her hand, and a hung-over-from-Christmas-Eve look on her face. Not much to choose from. Heavy sigh from my other half, we ordered soup and a roll, then quiche with salad. Boring, and no slurpy wine either, we looked forward to a glass of orange juice each.

Juice arrived first ~ complaint from husband it was not even fresh. I should have known this outing was not going well, but when the soup arrived, he nearly blew a gasket. (whatever that is!) SOUP? SOUP? "Looks like its been made in a baby burco boiler!!!" It did, and do you know, it tasted like it had. Plodding on, the roll came just before we were finishing the soup. "ROLL? ROLL?", he thundered, "this is a BAP, not a roll!" For SOUP?

Please don't ask me why I thought the Quiche would be hot, but it was straight from the fridge, if not the freezer, and believe me, it did nothing for his rising temper. Nor did the black bits on the unwashed lettuce! I tried to pass these off as extra fibre, but he was having none of it, and sent it back. Not a word of apology from the hung-over owner, who I thought was biding her time until she could hit the bottle after we had gone.

Conversation quite stilted between us during this fiasco, and he must have thought, whilst he was in a complaining mood, that I would be interested in his new socks. First time on that day, and finding great pleasure in letting me know how Marks and Spencer were totally useless in producing socks that were wearable. Trouser legs were rolled up for him to demonstrate and prove that during the technique he used to pull up his socks, two holes appeared either side of the hosiery. Imagine! Marks and Spencer with no quality control! Mood very low by this stage, and when the pudding menu arrived I took it upon myself to take hold of it before he tore it in two.

I couldn't face the thought of a coffee expose, and when the bill came it was wrong. (nooooh), but he loudly sorted it out with the lapsed AA member, and off we went. As we closed the door behind us, he turned to me and said "That was nice, we should do it again!" And he meant it!

I took him to the office for a coffee, and made it myself, not letting him see the milk carton from the 'fridge with the large white sticky label that said BREAST MILK. Stuck on to deter members of another office from using our milk, which they were prone to doing.

Happy as Larry when I got home, and flushed with success, he couldn't wait to tell his story. He had returned the offending socks to Marks and Spencer that afternoon, (still wearing them), lifting his leg and placing his foot onto the returns counter, enabling the assistant to see for herself how badly made they were. She was surprised at the display of leg, but took a deep breath and gave him a plastic bag in which to place his still-warm socks. Best of all, she presented him with a brand new pair, which he put on in front of her in case these, too, were faulty. All was well, and he turned to face the now quite long queue, most of them laughing at this very unusual man, he grinningly informed them "Now that's what I call customer service!"

You can be forgiven for thinking this happy mood would continue for the rest of the evening, but when the cat knocked the Christmas Angel off her perch, I had the perfect excuse to attack the brandy mince pies, washed down with a large helping of eggnog!!

Another Happy Christmas wrapped up!

IX
Do I Look Like A Cow?

Young and newly married (ish), we were posted to RAF Wildenrath in Germany, and had to spend 3 months in a RAF hotel-like establishment directly under the flight path of the Harrier Jump Jets. No vacant quarters to move into, and with no children, and husband away a good deal of the time, it was a good place to chill out and make friends with others in the same position. I lived a life of Riley ~ no cooking, cleaning, or washing up, and all meals provided. Not bad at age 25.

Loads of coffee mornings then, shopping trips, and sight-seeing excursions to while away the time, and the inevitable trip to the Bielefeld Flower Club!! A MUST for every budding Army wife, in fact, and there we spent our weekly get-togethers, complete with the requisite country-style basket ~ the Hermes scarf draped loosely over the shoulder in as fetching a way possible.

They even sold the must-haves at the club, to help any

woman who struggled to get THE LOOK. Must-haves being the baskets, of course, the said scarves, the leather shoulder-bags, the Regimental brooches, and packs of At-Home cards for the truly adventurous. The flowers and demonstrations were a secondary reason to visit the club, but if you were genuinely interested in the flowers, as I was, every available accessory for flower arranging was there for the buying.

We moved into quarters, and it wasn't long before I was pregnant with our eldest son. I quite liked being pregnant, and determined not to let it change me too much. By now, I had got a reputation for always being "dressed up", with not a hair out of place, even when gardening ~ and always with the slap on, of course. My mantra at the time was Look Efficient, Be Efficient, and the neighbours couldn't wait to see me balloon out over my feet, and slop around in dressing gown and slippers at lunch time! Not going to happen!!

I pushed myself too far of course, and at 8¾ months, was still having suppers at ours for 20 or so folks. Standing peeling and cooking and cleaning etc pre-party, and clearing up afterwards before flopping into bed at 3am was probably not too good an idea was it, but hey, undeterred, I snored away in my bed, happy with life.

I was awake at 8 am to get myself ready for the visit to the ante natal and relaxation class. Ha! I lay on the mattress on the floor, and with the midwife droning on and on, I fell fast asleep! For a full half hour! Midwife patting herself on the back 'cause it was her first relaxation class, and she had managed to get someone to drop off. She never knew the details of the last 24 hours!

Needless to say, they admitted me to hospital due to raised blood pressure and swollen ankles that I couldn't stand up on, and I prepared for child-birth. I say prepared ~ I did my nails and hair, and applied my make-up! By the time the birthing of my child was over (2 ½ days later), I looked like the wild woman of the Amazon ~ mascara smeared over my cheeks, hair on end and growing upwards, and eyes far too large for my grey and waxy face! Not pleasant! It was whilst I was in this state of utter shock and exhaustion, and staring blankly into space and wondering why I had got myself into this situation, that the nurse presented me with a baby. Mine! Thankfully cleaned up! She plucked up the courage to ask me if I was going to breast feed. "W-H-A-T?" - I thundered - "Do I look like a COW?" (For those of you who are reading this and know me, please do not answer).

Oh dear ~ being pregnant had been fun, and maybe I hadn't thought it through properly, but all this was very unexpected. Babies into the nursery, all new mums were then part of a regime in that RAF hospital, a regime that took up the whole day, and I was in for 12 days. Morning tea, baths, feeds, babies back to nursery and breakfast. Exercises. Feeds. Lunch. Another bath. Feeds. Bed for ½ hour, and then visitors (husbands to view babies through nursery window). Exercises, Feeds. Tea.1/2 hour on tummies. Feeds. Medication and bed. Repeat every day. With no variation.

Where was the time for hair and make-up? Not putting up with that, I pared off a bit here and a bit there, and by the time husbands appeared at visiting, I was fully manicured, and lipstick-perfect. I smiled and beamed, I was so pleased to see him, hoping he would realise what an almighty effort it had been, not to look like a slob. Reality was, that after viewing our baby through the nursery window, he promptly fell asleep in the chair, unable to keep awake after a full half hour drive! Hormones were careering all over my body, and they do funny things. Not being known to have temper tantrums, I selfishly thought it was ME that had had the biggest shock to my system, and I found myself harbouring nasty thoughts regarding the man who, up until now, I had wanted to spend the rest of my life with. He awoke to the sound of the bell, asking him to leave, and promised to stay awake during the next visits. A promise he tried hard to keep, but failed on several occasions.

Days of the tedious regime continued, and I got used to snatching time for hair etc ~ only thing was, a nurse came to see me ~ she had noticed I was always the last one to get my baby from the nursery, and the first to take him back! How to explain this away without Social Services becoming involved? Did she buy the reason I gave for trying to give my son time with me, whilst also needing time for myself to recover? Mothers having time to themselves was not on her nursie agenda, but to me it was vitally important.

I left hospital with a longed-for, and loved baby son, and MY batteries re-charged too, but I also left with a life-long nausea whenever I see mums breast-feeding! Or even talking about it! Seeing them plop a boob out in a restaurant is enough to send me running for the sick bucket, sorry folks ~ I am not your normal earth-mother am I?

My neighbours lost their bets during the next few months ~ I was always well turned out, whilst they continued to shop in the NAAFI, sometimes finding themselves in their fluffy slippers, and more worryingly, with the smeared mascara still evident from the day before. By the time my next baby boy came along we were in Malta, but even with the sunshine and blue Mediterranean the regime in the Royal Naval hospital was just the same. Not being as naïve as with my first one, this one was easier to take ~ well, up to the point where my baby son was a whacking 9lbs 13oz! Wow! I could easily get this one back to the nursery whilst the other mums were undoing their feeding bras!

Every time food was mentioned, he would wriggle and rustle about in his cot, seeming to know what we were talking about, and looking for-ever hungry. (He hasn't changed). As a joke my husband, who miraculously could keep awake this time round, brought in a Steak and Ale Pie, wrapped up in an enormous blue ribbon. All the other mums in the ward thought this a really good joke ~ we were used to having many, many belly laughs, even at the expense of their Caesarean stitches, and none of us minded the mascara smearing one little bit! I had fully trained them in looking efficient and being efficient). Unfortunately, I hadn't trained the nurse in the joke department.... the nurse who came to give me a talking-to about feeding my week old baby on solids!! The entire ward erupted into howls of more laughter, and I think she returned to her office feeling ever so slightly silly.

I left there feeling very refreshed and happy, and with the Carmen rollers firmly tucked under my arm, (and not a hair out of place). Baby being a bit on the heavy side, and therefore carried by my fit, and wide-awake soldier husband, along with my now 3 year old chatty eldest son. Happy days.

Baby number 3 came whilst we were in Birmingham, and so our daughter was born in a civilian hospital, with no daily regime! A breakthrough! I was to be induced, and have an epidural, and in 1977, not many of us were offered this rather unusual procedure, and the hospital were trialling it. Lucky me!! There I was, sitting up in bed, doing my nails, and the nurses telling me I was having contractions. What's not to like? Completely numb from the waist down, I couldn't get up to check my hair in the mirror, but they brought everything I needed to my bed. Make-up, brush etc, and a very good book I was keen to finish, and like the Queen of Sheba, I lounged there for a while and had my baby. Painlessly! No hair standing on end, no huge eyes and waxy face, and it had all seemed so easy. My daughter must have seen a much nicer face looking at her, than my sons had, and I apologise now to both boys for looking like a Halloween ghoul when they first saw me. I just KNOW they will read this and say "So what's changed?"

Back on the ward then, and with no regime to follow, but already a manicured and happy mum, the feeling of pins and needles in my legs told me the anaesthetic was wearing off. And who do you think came to see me? The consultant anaesthetist with a questionnaire in hand. I was asked ~ yes, asked ~ if I thought I had missed out on not having a natural child-birth!!!!! I told you it was a consultant, but you may have guessed by now that it was a male of the species. Only a man could ask that question!! Didn't he know that the only thing I missed out on was not being able to access the mirror on the opposite wall? Well, he may as well be told ~ you never know, he may have been able to rectify it if he saw fit.

2 little boys and their daddy picked us both up, brothers not taking their eyes off "her" for a second, and as I was about to leave the ward, oops ~ fluffy slippers or navy heels? A conundrum for ½ a second, and of course, the heels won.

PS: Now nearing 80, and fending off dementia as best I can, I know that when I am found wandering the streets in my nightie, I will probably have opted for the fluffy slippers ~ (unintentionally), ~ and for family and friends, please borrow my book on Contented Dementia ~ I will rest easy knowing you will understand my muddled state, and keep me happy (ish). And I won't need a mirror!! Or a brush!! Or mascara!! ~ or perhaps I will!!

X

Random Thoughts

Have been mulling over the past years, searching my tired brain for something that might amuse you. I use the singular, due to there possibly being only one single person who may just be interested in the minutia of my life, and if you are that person, I applaud you for your tenacity in following my "Volumes of a once-productive Life".

I say productive ~ because that's how I feel it was, what with a husband, 3 children, and now 7 grandchildren, and I can say with hand on heart that I am extremely proud of each and every one. Even if that was all I had achieved, it would feel like a life well-spent, but in and around it all, I have managed to share some great, great memories with friends from the various countries we have lived in, have had SO many laughs with them, have entertained, and been entertained and have hopefully improved the lot of some of the people I have worked with in my working life. Oh heavens, this is sounding far too serious, just know that if you are one of these people, ~ and you know who you are ~ I wholeheartedly apologise! Shoot me now, and don't give me a second thought, just be glad you got out relatively unscathed!! Or did you??

Don't think I got out unscathed from my in-laws really, what with the sharp tongues and all, and the rolling eye-balls. Come to think of it, that sounds like ME with THEM, not the other way round though ~ perhaps ~ perhaps I was just as bad!!! Mind you, there was a particular time when we arrived back from a posting from the back-of-beyond, ~ sorry, Canada, that my mother in law did get a dose of Karma. We arrived back in UK at Brize Norton after a few days of travelling, a 7 hour flight, customs checks, and organising for us to collect a new car at the airport on our return. 7 year old daughter in tow, very tired, very anxious, and short on the patience thing. Our in-laws met us at the airport, and we all started on the 3 hour drive to their house ~ we were to stay with them for a while before we took over our new quarters in Germany.

Daughter very hungry, tired, crabby and thirsty as we arrived at their house and not wanting the cooing we had to do regarding in-laws new carpet!! A very red carpet. Newly laid for our return. Several asks for water went un-responded-to, until a fractious Granny offered her some Ribena to shut her up. It was winter and extremely cold, (we had come from Canada where it was minus 18 degrees in September!) but

Granny still gave her hot Ribena!! Would not entertain a cold one as it was winter (?), not even when our daughter wailed she hated hot Ribena ~ instead Granny stood over her to make sure she drank it all up!! Daughter did as she was told, and not more than 3 minutes later, vomited it up all over the new Axminster!! I said it was a red carpet, but unfortunately for the in-laws, was not the same red as Ribena vomit. It seemed like a long visit.

Completely unrelated ~ but that's how my mind works when I am thinking ~ that same daughter, now grown up and with 2 boys of her own, (4 and 7 at the time) was driving to see us one day when she found herself behind a dithery woman driver at a roundabout. Don't think my daughter has dithered in her life, and as this ditherer in front of her let one car after another go round the roundabout, daughter said in a rather loud voice "for goodness sake ~ grow a pair"!!! A little voice from the back seat shouted, "Yeah ~ and grow an apple too"!!

Being stationed in Malta in the 70s, was good fun all round, and my husband was in charge of the team that provided and serviced telephones and telephone cable for Army and Navy on the Island. I might have got that wrong, and if I have, no doubt he will delight in telling me so, but that is how I saw his job. When the Royal Naval ships came into the harbour, the team provided underwater cables for their telephones. Quite a feat of engineering, and the team worked well (some Maltese, some British Army), but guess who got the invites to the ships parties? Yes, my lovely husband and his plus one!!

When Ark Royal arrived on a very windy and blustery visit, the cables were provided, and the invite followed for a party on board for husband and me. Yayyy! The sea was VERY choppy, and the usual walk-way couldn't be used, and so they provided the Admirals barge for the visitors to be taken from harbour to ship, anchored away from the dockside itself. Well, that part ok, and then we found out that the Navy are brilliant at hosting parties, and we stood on the flight deck, in the fresh sea air, drinking Horses Necks. Brandy and Ginger to us. The whole of the flight deck lit up, and the whole of my face followed suit, and everyone had far too many of those Horses Necks, and as the daylight dimmed to dusk, the flight deck began to move, Downwards! Took me a while to realise what was happening, it was surreal to be going slowly downwards, into the bulk of the ship. We arrived on the lower level, and the party continued as the ceiling closed over us. Quite a bit of partying, and then I needed the loo. I was shown the way to a step-ladder, which I had to climb, in order to use the "heads" (toilets). Oh dear. Too much brandy, and too many rungs on that ladder, but up I lurched, and for those who know me, there would have been a lot of noise, and the sight would not have been a good one for any unsuspecting sailor who happened to pass by. Relieved, I then had to come down again ~ just use your imagination at this point!! I bear no grudges to the sailor who tried to help me!!!

Time to go home then, and as the sea was calm(er), my husband's men had laid on a wooden walk-way that sat on the surface of the sea, yes, on the surface of the sea, all the way back to the harbour, and we all had to hang on to ropes as we navigated our way, inch by inch along this moving walk-way! So YES ~ I HAVE WALKED ON WATER!!!

Again, I ramble around the thing I call a brain, and remember the Candle shop we owned in York, and a customer of the arrogant persuasion. I was serving her, along with one of our young staff, and we had both jumped through hoops to please this pushy customer. She LOVED having us run around to keep her happy, and after seemingly endless fuss, settled on a glass vase. She flung her arm in the general direction of the said vase, of which there was a choice of 2 colours. One plain see-through glass, and the other a dark red, and the flow of her arm gave us no indication which of the 2 she had condescended to buy. When I asked for clarification, she said "the wine coloured one", in a rather out-of-patience way. I couldn't resist, and asked, "would that be the Claret, or the Chardonnay?". We prided ourselves on Customer Service!!

Talking of awkward customers, my mother was one of the worst, and long before her dementia kicked in, she was prone to using her walking stick to point in the direction of the assistants in her local shops. Pointing, as in aggressively shoving it in their faces!! It was almost our 25th wedding anniversary, and my sister was roped in to take her shopping for a suitable present for us. Sister asked what we would like, and a piece of Ainsley China was agreed upon. We were collecting the odd pieces at the time. Sister took out an Insurance Policy in readiness for this shopping trip, which she dreaded, owing to my mother's reputation for eating assistants alive!! She was almost prepared, but not quite! Whittakers Store in Bolton, was the only good department store in a 20 mile radius. and off they set with my sister hyperventilating as they approached the doors to this most pleasant store. They asked for Ainsley China, and were shown to the correct area. My mother chose to sit down, resting both hands on the handle of her walking stick, whilst my sister browsed. Sue pointed out some pieces, but NO! Too small!! She went a little larger," NO!! You have no idea!!" Tut-tutting as she realised my sister was as useless as she had thought, and pointing at the assistant who thought she was about to knock some of the china over! She banged her stick loudly on the floor, to get my sister's attention, seeing as she had spotted the very thing!!! A very large fruit bowl, raised on 3 tiny feet. Ainsley, and perfect. She wanted it. She shouted to my sister that she wanted it, and she pointed the stick at the assistant to inform her that yes, she wanted it. She told the assistant that of course she would want a box, as it was for her other daughter's Silver Wedding, and off she was dispatched to bubble-wrap it and box it. Whilst that was going on, my sister thought to ask our mother if she knew how much it was, only to be shouted down by mother, saying "if you need to ask the price, you shouldn't be shopping in this store!!!!"

Sister shut up. Assistant returned, and my mother tut-tutted as it wasn't gift wrapped, and she asked for it to be wrapped in Ainsley wrapping paper. Assistant obliged. Now remember this was over 30 years ago. The wrapped box was sitting in front of my mother, when the assistant rang it into the till, informing my mother that there was £300 to pay!! Quick as a flash, mother said, "I think she already has one thank you", and she used her stick for support as she marched out of the store. Sister running behind her, and with a very red face! Mother moved really fast for someone who used a walking stick, but not as fast as my sister with her straight, angry back as she headed back to the car!!

I am beginning to remember other goings-on, but the clock is telling me that bed-time has gone long ago. Perhaps I will remember them in the morning, but I don't hold out much hope of that one!!

Morning after. Nope, can't remember a thing!!

XI
Casualty

I love hospitals. I love the smell, I love the atmosphere (mostly) and I love the corridors leading to ~ well ~ who knows where? There is a certain feeling of being cocooned in a bubble of activity, especially if you work in one.......

I DID work in one! I was on reception in the Casualty Department, after answering an ad in the local paper. Well, I thought, I watch Casualty every week, and it looked OK to me, so nothing ventured, I had applied.

I turned up for the interview and joined the queue!! About 12 candidates were already in the queue, and more arriving as I waited my turn. Hell ~ I glanced at all those before me (young and efficient-looking), and thought, "No chance here for me then!" I was torn between staying and being humiliated, or legging it back home and cursing myself. That, and being seen by my husband as a quitter! Fight, or flight? I began to look the young things over as I edged towards the front of the queue, and saw that not many had clean shoes! And their bags didn't match anything! AND they were leaning on the wall! Tut-Tut!

Of course I decided to fight, and I was edging slowly towards the front of the queue, and after careful consideration of my opponents, I still thought the fight would be lost, and the job would elude me.

Finally, I was ushered into the interview room. There sat HR lady, with her mate who I assumed was one of her minions, and who obviously did not enjoy her job one bit judging by the set-in-concrete-frown. It crossed my mind that now I understood exactly why their department was called Human Remains, instead of Human Resources! Alongside her, was the Nursing Sister from Casualty, (Or A&E as it is now) looking very confrontational.

Various normal ish questions from HR lady, and probing ones from her mate with the frown. (Who, I wondered had interviewed her and asked her what she could bring to the job?). I coped with all their questions and then it was the turn of the stern, nearing-retirement Nursing Sister. I turned to face her. "What would you do if a man came in to Casualty, covered in blood, with a chain-saw stuck in his shoulder?" Her steely blue eyes piercing directly into my soul. "I would sit him down if he hadn't already fallen, and try to get his name and address before he fainted, and get a medic as soon as possible" I said. Those eyes changed from steel blue, to sunny-sky- blue, and she stood up with arms raised towards the heavens and shouted "Hallelujah!"

I got the job!!! And found out later that everyone else had said they would take the chain-saw out!! Can't believe it, can you? Well, actually I could ~ their dirty shoes said it all.

After a month training in Medical Records (just loved all those files ~ so many lives tied up in them all), I was let loose on an unsuspecting public. I had my ID photo done by the frowning HR lady, who incidentally, had my card with new photo, and as she came to hand it to me she asked "Is this yours?" Who else could it POSSIBLY have been for?

We did have fun, surprisingly, and the team were great. The sister who interviewed me was fantastic ~ definitely of the old school of nursing. Strict but fair with staff, but by golly, her patients got the best she could give them! I saw her once as an ambulance brought in a patient who had caught his leg in machinery. There she was, a few moments later, emerging from the ambulance, elbowing everyone out of her way, and with his severed leg tucked firmly under her arm!! She was quite a character, and I had great respect for her. We got on well, but as the department went into computerisation (much to her disgust), she was finally defeated by it. She fought tooth and nail at many many meetings, to have the old ledger system back, but to no avail. She was right ~ it took twice as long to book someone in, and twice as long to make referrals to fracture clinics etc, and the computer was always crashing. She never got the hang of it ~ I tried to talk her through it on many occasions, but she finally gave in and retired to her garden. A loss to all her patients, and the staff who would do anything for her. PROGRESS!!!!!!

The first week the computers were installed, we were all

apprehensive. Every patient who visits A&E has a letter sent to their GP, and the computer asks for codes to signify why the patient was there, the treatment given, and discharge details. NOW! We were all new to these codes, all the staff, including nurses and doctors, and we all had turns on trying to input the correct information. The letters that came out of the other end of the wretched computer went direct to the GP, as a normally worded letter. Seemed that during that first week, someone(?) had sent a letter advising that a patient had had a plaster cast to his head following a hand injury, and had been hospitalised for 3 months intensive physiotherapy!!! I know what you are thinking! It must have been me!! Go on ~ admit it. I am saying nothing.

There was a rush on when several ambulances brought in workers from a pig farm that had been on fire. No serious injuries ~ just lots of blackened pig farmers lying in cubicles, being checked over and discharged. One of the nurses asked why I was spraying air freshener around the desk area when they left. "To get rid of the pork scratchings smell ~ it's making me hungry" I said!!

The doctors had a good sense of humour too. They knew I couldn't say the F word. Or the P word ~ you know ~ the dangly bit thingy. The V word gave me trouble too (front bottom), and so they all used the words to the Nth degree if they could. They knew their scrawly writing would give me trouble, and so they scrawled even scrawlier so I would have to ask them before coding on the computer. I always blushed bright red, and they always laughed at me!! Cruel lot!

Funny how some things and some people stay in the memory box. One family certainly did. The mother was brought in by her son. Mother in cubicle, when another son arrived. Then another. Then 2 daughters and their children, and before you knew it, aunts and uncles were circling too! They took up the whole of the waiting area ~ mother OK by the way ~ and several had brought flasks of tea with them, seemingly ready for a vigil. All extremely worried for the matriarch of the family, and some tearful. I answered the phone, and a voice said "How's mi mam?" I just knew who he meant!!

I left after a year to do what I had wanted to do for some time. Work for Social Services. Whilst there, I had, on occasions, to speak on the phone to GP's on behalf of my clients, ~ some of the doctors knew me from working in A&E when I was there. Several times, when speaking about a client, they would ask about the V word, or the P word, to wind me up and I wish, I wish I could have very politely told them to **** Off, but I couldn't. Product of a repressed childhood!!!

I have to apologise at this point if my grandchildren are reading this. It doesn't look good if their Grandma was considering using that dreadful language, but I swear that word has never ever passed my lips.....no matter WHAT my daughter says!!!!

XII
Curly Whirly Baby

Young Officers are not well known for their common sense, or indeed for their sharp incisive clarity of thought. We all knew that, but hoped they would learn quickly (some of them even did), but not all!

As a Squadron Commander (Major) in charge of a variety of Army ranks, including the said young-wet-behind-the-ears officers, my husband was enjoying his job, and was especially grateful to his Sgt Major ~ a broad Glaswegian disciplinarian, heavy drinking, yet good-hearted, and who took no prisoners! He had to salute the young officers and address them as 'Sir', but I could always detect a slight snarl on the 'Sir' bit ~ and yet he would do anything for my husband, and they got on well. Rumour had it he had been a naughty boy in the past ~ probably taking no nonsense from his soldiers, his lumpy face showing scars from battles not fought on the battlefield, but behind many a pub.

He had learned to curb his enthusiasm for a fight, and had quite an important job within the Squadron, not least in the disciplining of his soldiers! He was strict when needed, but I have seen him and his wife, along with myself and my husband, helping out families who were struggling, and between us we kept the morale as high as it could be.

Although I say this myself, I ran a really good Wives' Club. We enjoyed our time together, and I once took 20 wives to Berlin for a weekend away from the children, at a time when the Berlin Wall was still in place. We ran auctions ~ I had a Volvo estate and filled it with things to sell ~ coming home with 3 car loads that I couldn't resist buying!! We went shooting on the ranges, the soldiers taking all our children on treasure hunts in the woods whilst we learned to shoot pistols and rifles. I came second overall, and have no idea how!! And my husband had soldiers from other Squadrons, applying to join ours because their wives had heard about our club. All in all, a really good time!

Sgt Major happened to have his own office, and of course his own filing cabinet, and sitting in the top drawer was his Teddy! Must have been a cuddly one once, but now it was dog-eared ~ stuffing coming out, no arm, and really-really filthy!! When he was angry (and he could be VERY angry), he woke up the teddy and smashed it around the office, shouting expletives, growling at it, and thumping it until he felt better!! Not good for the mute teddy, but better than the guard-room for Sgt Major, and he would close the drawer on Teddy with a very large grin on his face!! Job done!!

I always visited any of the Squadron wives when they had their babies ~ took them flowers and choccies etc,~ and coo cooed over their little darlings. Not my favourite things, babies, had trouble with my own, but someone else's were a whole new ball game. Still, you do your best, and I didn't have to pick them up if I didn't want to, so I could manage a few minutes making all the right noises.

Sgt Major rang me to let me know of a new arrival in the maternity ward, but said one of the young Officers' had already visited that day. I couldn't go then, but arranged for a visit the day after. Before I went to gawp at baby, I went to see the afore-mentioned Officer, for a bit of info. "Oh my Lord," he said, "I didn't know where to look!" He told me that the baby was disabled, with very, very long legs, curling round in the bottom of the cot, and crying loudly. Mum was spaced out, and he thought she couldn't accept the baby as it was.

I didn't waste any more time, off I went on my mission to see this young, first-time mum, and planning what to say to her as I sped along the autobahn. I arrived trying to put on my most "positive" face, and went to meet them both, flowers in hand. Calm mum, just had a rest, and looking very excited at having her baby, and as usual, wanted me to pick her up! "This is it" I thought, and I lifted the baby out of her cot. For a baby, she was a nice-ish one, and I took a deep breath and sat down. We talked about the birth (they always insist on telling you every awful detail of the horrors they had been through) ~ it's then I sometimes feel quite faint ~ I look like I am an Earth Mother, but I am far from it!! At least at the baby stage. I am alright when they can talk.

I cuddled and cooed, and very surreptitiously, felt the baby's legs. I opened the baby nightgown at the bottom, and pretended to love babies feet, which I unearthed from the folds of the gown. Perfect! No problems. Baby back to mum, she gave her a cuddle and placed her back in the cot, coiling the long nightgown into a snake-like curl!!!! (like long legs)!!

I went straight back to Sgt Major, and laughed till I ached with him. As I walked down the corridor, I heard his filing cabinet drawer opening, and worried for the fate of his teddy. Another young Officer to have to train in baby recognition!

We had lots of parties. And they took a deal of planning, usually between the two of us, but one time my husband just didn't have the time to give me for the planning. I am meticulous to the Nth degree (or was), but every time I brought up the subject of the blessed "do", he glazed over, and went back to whatever it was that needed greater attention. I knew he was nice and thoughtful to everyone else, and so I formed a cunning plan.

I rang his office and asked if he could possibly see one of the Squadron wives the day after. -Just for half an hour-. "Of course" he said, "who is it?" "She would rather not say, but is 2pm ok?" That evening he asked again, and I told him it was personal, and that I would come with her. This seemed to satisfy my incredibly busy man.

2pm the day after, I knocked on his office door, pen and pad in hand, and waited. He opened the door and I smelled the coffee ~ my goodness ~ and he peered over my shoulder. "Where is she?" I entered, and shut the door. "Right, pour the coffee then, I only have half an hour ~ how many bottles of wine do I need for 18 etc etc?" It worked!! I shook hands with him at 2.30 and thanked him for his time!!

We left after 2 very happy years, and were 'dined out' of various clubs and messes. The Sergeants' Mess gave us a great send-off, and the Sergeant Major presented us with 6 whisky glasses (his favourite tipple) on a silver salver. He would not hand it over until I had sung Rule Britannia!! Have you ever heard me sing? It sounds like a pig in labour. Like nothing you have ever heard before ~ even my music teacher told me to mime after many attempts to make me melodic! It brings tears to a hardened ear, but I did it (or attempted to) and there were many many tears that evening. Tears of disbelief, of sorrow, and of course, laughter. And as I sat down, salver and glasses in hand, I noticed Teddy, peering from behind the port decanter! Oh dear ~ that dog-eared wretch would be in for it again, later!! Too much wine, too much beer for their mess to cope with, and of course, the inevitable inebriated sots who would wake up the next day, unaware of another Teddy- mauling going on in the filing cabinet. Happy days!!

XIII
Freedom At Last....

I was relatively late learning to drive. Well, ~ 30! My husband had tried to teach me, when we were first married, about 200 years ago, but when I drove into a hedge instead of steering right at a T junction, his short temper showed its ugly head and I got out of the car as best I could and stomped off. Don't know where I thought I was going ~ we were in the Yorkshire Dales with only sheep for company, but I think it was the first time I realised I didn't like being told what to do. Luckily he caught up with me, and with gorse sticking to the bumper of our little Beetle car, words were spoken regarding my inability to steer! What a fuss!

I didn't try again until we were living in Malta, with a 2 year old son and pregnant with our 2nd one. NOW ~ in Malta, everyone drives on the side of the road that's in the shade, and with the pot-holes being what they were.......it was a rough ride!!

I got on OK and my Maltese instructor put me in for my test. Had to meet at a disused airfield at 5 am.-.5 am!!..- With a horde of other examinees and their instructors. The test, believe it or not, took the form of a 100 yard drive, then reversing between 2 tar barrels, and finally, parallel parking. All fine until the reversing, when the car bumped the tar barrel, so instant failure!! Head down, I had to own up to my instructor, who said, "You had £5 in your purse? You give him money, he pass you"!! Silly me!! Upshot was ~ I had to return the following week, and this time I passed. I now had an International (!) Driver's Licence, and on my return to UK I could drive for 1 year before I had to take a UK test. Freedom!

No more waiting for buses, no more waiting for lifts, and 1 week later, I drove my pregnant self to a Wives Club committee meeting at a friend's house.

New to this driving lark, I pulled up in front of friend's garage, and oh heck! There are 2 pedals to choose with the right foot, and I chose the wrong one, and the car made a bee-line for my friend's garage door, giving it a very fetching caved-in look, and at the same time doing some damage to our car. Couldn't stand around, I had a meeting to attend, so off I went and socialised, drank coffee, and planned what it was we had to plan. Prioritising!

Time to leave, and it was then I owned up to my friend about her dented garage door. Horrified that I hadn't mentioned it sooner, and thinking I was crackers for sitting there all morning possibly in shock, we went to assess the damage. "Don't worry about the door" I laughed (pregnant) "John will come round tonight to fix it!" She thought I shouldn't drive, she thought I should be checked out by a medic, in fact, she was stressing after seeing the bashed-in bonnet with the headlight hanging out and dangling for all to see. Good Heavens! I was thinking, a bit of an over-reaction to a small dent!!

I insisted on driving home, and during the drive I remember having a strict conversation with myself about what I would say to the man who tells me what to do. Well, he tells me what to do so many times, I choose when to listen, and the conversation in my head was along the lines of "well I don't care what he says...I am pregnant, 6 months to be exact, and HE does silly things WITHOUT hormones running amok" Oh and "I have only just passed my test". I decided to just be matter-of-fact, and show no emotion, which I didn't have anyway.

Once home, I picked up the phone and dialled my husband's number. "Hello" said a very lovely kind voice......and I reacted by sobbing and blubbering. Pathetic!!

After this fiasco, and with my baby safely born and now 6 months old, you couldn't keep me in. I was always driving round the Island, shopping, and mixing with friends for coffee, and one friend in particular was rather fond of her Sherry Mornings!!! With husband looking after my/our 2 children off I went for one of these 10.30 am get-togethers. Had a great time, lots of laughs and eats, the sherry turned to Pimms, and I offered 3 other friends a lift home. (Get me!) Laughing loudly as we went heading along the pock-marked roads, with the Mediterranean shining deep blue, and turquoise, and without a care in the world, I felt like Isadora Duncan. But in a Ford Escort!!

Then ~ in my rear view mirror, I saw the Military Police indicating for me to pull over. I did. "Oooooh, have I been going too fast?" I said, eyes very very wide. "Can I ask where you have been?" asked a Corporal, smelling my breath. "I've only been to a sherry morning" I giggled. He very slowly, too slowly I thought, pulled his wrist in front of my face in a rather theatrical manner to look at his watch, and staring straight into my eyes, informed me it was 10 to 6!!   Whoops!!

XIV
Hobbies

I have never seen the sense in hobbies, I like making things, creating things, but the obsession that comes with a hobby, has passed me by. My husband though has been obsessed with various hobbies, from Photography to Model Aircraft making and flying, and now his computing. The photography lasted a few years, when the best (that means expensive) equipment had to be owned, and where ~ if we had a spare room ~ (even a spare toilet) he transformed into a darkroom. No one allowed to enter of course, for fear of losing prints, and there he spent hours, days, weeks, presiding over gurgling trays of foul-smelling liquid like a mad scientist. On his own, in the dark, and once, in a cellar room for the whole of the Easter holiday. Mostly without food, and forgive me, also without a thought for his family! Except that the photos were mostly the children (well, he needed to recognise them!). Oh, and plants and flowers ~ we had heaps of photos of flowers, close-ups of dew drops on them, rain on them, sun on them, and the fireworks......! Whenever I caught up with hubby for the odd cuppa, the chemical aroma preceded him and his pallor got ever more pallid. Enough!!

Cameras packed away, we moved to Catterick, where he took to building model aircraft. Large ones. He had started this hobby a few years earlier, and still had the carcasses of aircraft packed away in boxes, and with a friend of his who was also obsessed with this pastime (?), began to build.

Both families lost their dining rooms to Balsa Wood, and the detritus that model building inexorably brings with it: - Paints, oils, batteries, wire. engine bits and grubby smelly rags, all laid out on a dining room table with orders not to touch. 6 foot wing spans were normal, and I even saw a model, smiling pilot, sitting on my chair! I didn't smile, the mess was dreadful ~ and for anyone who knows us, will know the kind of mess my husband can make, and what he likes to surround himself with. Mess on top of mess.

Finally, a finished plane! With pride oozing out of every pore, he placed it on the front lawn to have it's photo taken from every conceivable angle. Ready for its maiden flight at last, hubby went indoors to watch a football match on the telly ~ that daft one from Wembley ~ with a cup. A cup final, but it never is, is it? Final I mean!

He got together the Radio control, and went out for the plane. No plane!! Nothing!! Well, he was beside himself as he ran around the garden, round the back garden, then leapt over the hedge to the neighbours garden, face contorted in grief. Up and down the road he went, cursing through his clenched teeth ~ then he rang the Police. Thankfully not 999, but the local Bobby came with his notebook at the ready for a statement re the theft. Of a model plane. He promised to find it. Red with anger, my usually calm (!) husband did not believe him, but resigned himself to grieving alone, in the Bermuda Triangle that was Catterick Garrison. And then he saw a vision! A few anxious hours after the Bobby had left on his mission, he came to call again, and this time with the plane, which had a smashed-in tail. 2 small boys had dragged it along the road and finally left it in the field after being unable to do anything with this monster. My husband tried not to hug the Bobby, but the relief.........!!   He set-to and repaired the damage, and a few days later headed to the field for the long-awaited flight. I saw him return home with a satisfied smile on his face ~ and with the plane in 4 plastic bags!! Broken bits protruding in all directions. "Oh well he said, "back to the drawing board!"

Weeks of effort went by...............

Then, one sunny Sunday he put the lawn mower and plane

into the car. Lawn Mower???? Yes, he was hoping to mow the Yorkshire Moors in order to make a runway!! (Don't ask)

Friend and Hubby headed off to the moors along with the mower, and selected aircraft, and my jaw dropped for at least 5 minutes. Well, until I saw the dining room that is, and then I think I lost it!! I piled all the dross, the batteries, the oil, the paint, the rags, and all things boyish onto a large board he used, and placed it strategically on the front drive! My intention was for him to reverse over it as he came home! And flatten it!!

A bit later I called my friend (the wife of his friend), who tried to talk me out of it due to the rumbling thunder, and downpour due any minute. I did feel bad for a bit ~ I don't know why, cause I was hoping it would soon be under the car ~ so I covered the pile with plastic covers. I cleaned the dining room. He came home. He reversed like he always did, but saw the pile, and steered around it. DAMN!! In he came, "Been tidying up then?" he asked, smiling.

The furniture-making craze didn't last that long really, (no lathe involved) but was horrendous during the carpentry. For some unfathomable reason, he convinced himself that our dining room/aircraft hangar, was the perfect workshop, and after seeing a Chippendale piece on Antiques Roadshow, he began to fashion his own variation. Wood was delivered, was sawn and hammered, fitted and tweaked. Weeks went by. The woody smell was, I have to say, very pleasant. An electric saw was in full swing when I entered, and a cloud of woody dust met me, and covered the whole room. Ornaments, light-fittings, windows and plants were coated, as, unconcerned he worked on. "Soon be finished" was all he could say.

The sanding and waxing followed, then another fine sanding, and varnishing, and waxing again – and we were both pleased with the result. Lovely. Phone call from my mother and father, who were asking to call the following day, so HELL...lots to do! Tools out! Mess to garage, and sideboard standing proud. I stayed up until 2 am that night, I cleaned and polished everything in that dining room from the light-fittings to the door knobs, even cleaning the leaves on the dusty plants. Then I polished it all, and fell into bed exhausted!!

I woke with the alarm at 7 ~ husband already up, and as I pottered about upstairs I could hear a noise that I just knew I had heard before - recently. I legged it to the dining room. He still had the sander in his hand, and as I choked on the dust he said, "Oh, morning, thought I would give it another going-over!" I didn't cry, as such, I remember a wail coming out of my throat, and I remember looking for something heavy to...... well, not really sure WHAT!! It was lucky for him that my parents arrived before I throttled him. My dad would have forgiven him anything, but my mother was made of sterner stuff, and with a sharper tongue. My husband knew how to manage her, ~ a coffee laced with liqueur did the trick!

The computer stage has lasted longer than most of his pastimes, and incidentally has taken up most time. Thankfully, it's a fairly quiet and clean operation, but it definitely IS an obsession. I saw him huddled over a laptop in the car during a picnic in the woods the other day, desperately seeking WIFI activity!!!

What next?

XV
Greensleeves

We found ourselves in Bristol ~ husband still in the Army ~ and this time as Training Major for the TA. A really, really good posting for many reasons, location, job, social life, and for me, my first job in 100 years.

I answered an ad in the local paper for an Activities Organiser. Not clear from the ad who the organising was for, but I thought as I had been organising activities for Army Wives for the past 20 years, I would give it a try.

Interview was going well. My interviewer was a lovely man nearing retirement age himself, and who owned up-market Residential Homes and Nursing Homes in a beautiful part of Bristol. The homes were elegant Georgian buildings set in lovely gardens near to a leafy Common. His clientèle included retired business men, wealthy widows, and the odd Lord or Lady, who until recently had been used to "dressing for dinner". Could I drive a mini-bus? It is here I own up to having lied through my front teeth! Well, not outright lies, but I believe I said something about taking Army Wives out in a mini-bus. I had, but I forgot to tell him that someone else did the driving. I got the job!!

Residents lived in suites ~ sitting room, bedroom, bathroom and kitchenette, and it seemed they stayed in there for most of the day except for meals, when they used the dining room for dining, but not for talking much to each other.

It was here I met my friend for the next 30 or so years. She was the Assistant Matron, and I never met a resident or member of staff who had a bad word to say about her. The residents mutually adored her, but all wanted a lot from her in their individual ways, and she gave it to them.

I practised driving the mini-bus. I did flower-arranging once a week, and one by one the residents started to join in as we discussed news items, books etc, whilst I wrestled with the roses and lilies, and Betty helped serve the coffee. Then came the outings. They made trips to the music room so they could put their name on the Outings List, and whilst they were there, we played Whist and discussed the next trip in the bus. We went to Weston-super-Mare, had picnics at Tintern Abbey, rides around the countryside, and occasionally came to my house for coffee. When they complained of a draught in the bus, I organised them into a knitting group where they knitted squares and sewed them together into knee blankets to keep them warm. Couth knee blankets you understand ~ all colour co-ordinated, and when they got on the bus I allocated a blanket to match the clothes they were wearing. They loved it!

On one outing they bought straw boaters to wear at the garden party I organised for them, and where they got slightly tipsy on half a glass of Bristol Cream! I loved it all, and enjoyed seeing them mix with one another, and it never felt like "work".

The owner and his wife became friends of ours, and when I received a request from two entertainers to do a musical afternoon, they straight away trusted my judgement. They were wrong to!!! I had cleared it with the musicians ~ NO ~ the residents would definitely not like a sing-along, or even music from the musicals. I asked if they could do light classical ~ maybe Greensleeves, something like that. Oh yes!! They could do that easily. I booked them!! And paid their £50 fee up front.

Most residents looked forward to it. I looked forward to it. The staff looked forward to it, and the cook made special cakes for the afternoon tea we were having prior to the concert. The tea was served and the ladies in their finery sat around in anticipation. In came a resident commonly known as "the Duchess". An elegant lady, bedecked in her finest floating afternoon dress, and set off to perfection by her (very large) diamonds. (She owned an original Lowry). Now, she didn't often come out of her suite of rooms, but here she was, on the front row, being as music was "her thing", and gracing everyone with her powerful presence.

And then the musicians arrived!! I use the term musician loosely. They were two men in gold and black waistcoats, one with an electric keyboard, the other with a banjo. They made an impressive entrance 'cause they tripped badly coming into the music room ~ not so much due to the step, more because they had been in the pub since 11.

They had forgotten I had said no to sing-along and they started with "My Old Man's a Dustman". I stopped them. Then came Sound of Music (of sorts) I stopped them, and reminded them of our conversation and the need for light classics. I regretted getting near to them, the smell of beer was over-whelming, but they tried Greensleeves (after a fashion). It was the only classical (?) music they knew, and so they played it, over and over till I stopped them. At this stage they were thinking the residents hadn't had their moneys' worth, and thought to tell a few jokes!!

One of them stood in front of the Duchess, and told them all that he was surrounded by beautiful ladies, and horror of horrors, here he was without his weekend "pack of three"!!!!!! Oh Lord. Silence. The Duchess shuffled to her full height, steadying herself on her zimmer frame and said, "I hope he isn't going to smoke!".....and left. A pack of cigarettes obviously more nauseating to her than missing condoms!

It was at this point I asked them to leave, in fact, I helped them gather their belongings together, and as I went into the hall, I saw the staff en masse, bent two double, tissues to their eyes, and trying and not succeeding to stifle their laughter. Mortified just doesn't cover it.

My friend the Assistant Matron went round to the ones still shell-shocked and gave out the chocolates to raise blood sugar, and we raffled off the many flower arrangements from around that room which had been placed to welcome the music. (!)

The Duchess was still muttering about the "common" smokers the following day, but with memory failing, thank goodness did not hold a grudge for long.

My friend still remembers, and still reminds me, but I remember her, and a hangover, and an Army church! Another story.........!

XVI
In-Laws

We clashed! That's the top and bottom of it! Well, at least my mother-in-law and me did. I took her son away, came from a grimy town, and I didn't know the difference between an oak tree and a primrose (according to them both), so I was on a sticky wicket from the get-go. The taking of their son was my biggest fault and I never got them over that heinous crime for the rest of their lives.

To be fair, I never liked their countryside, or their way of life, and I could never raise the enthusiasm to rush squealing to the window to watch a hedgehog trotting across the lawn. I had only ever seen one with a tyre mark across it's back, and I never remember rushing to a window to catch a glimpse.

Now I was the sort of young wife who donned the make-up and did my hair before starting the gardening! I liked the theatre, ballet, and went to concerts about 4 times a year (no not the Beatles ~ I disliked them ~ orchestral music I mean). My friends did the same. Ok, I HAD been to the country before, but usually in a car and hadn't often got out of the car except to take a photo. This walking along the lanes and smelling for foxes didn't thrill me over-much, and consequently, I got a lot of stick from my in-laws. Especially as I didn't even own a pair of wellies. No cars going past their house, no people, no gossip, no shops, no life! I must have been a nightmare for them.

I grew up LIVING in a shop, for goodness sake, and remember standing in a drawer behind the counter, at age 4, helping my dad to serve the customers. By the time I was 21 I was managing a shop with 4 staff, so NO, leaves did not, neither do they now, have an appeal for me.

If I was a nightmare for them, they got their own back in many ways, disapproving and tut-tutting when I cooked for them, and I have seen them limp in seemingly excruciating rheumatic pain as they complained about damp bedding when they stayed with us. Even after explaining the sheets had their home in the airing cupboard! Every house we ever lived in they seemed to dislike if I liked it, until I thought HAH!! When we moved to a lovely house in Bristol, I complained to them I wasn't happy with it ~ low and behold ~ they loved it!!

It was in this sort of confrontational set-up that this story is told.

They had stayed with us for 2 weeks in our home in Germany ~ 2 whole weeks! Children at school every day, and we all know what that is like in the morning with homework still being finished, socks to match up, and the inevitable from second son ~ "Mu-um, I need a fancy dress for assembly!" Loud angry voice from upstairs "we haven't had our cup of tea yet!!" (She was used to a "Teas-Made" back home).

Every day was a sight-seeing trip, except they didn't get a move on in the morning, and so by the time we did, I had them moving in too big a rush as the children needed to be picked up early afternoon. (I suffered from a great deal of indigestion).

The sight-seeing trips around Germany, although rushed, still reminded them of the War. The countryside disappointed them (what a way to farm.. no hedges!) and what with the rheumatics and funny food, I personally think they were glad to be going home. I felt the same.

On their last night with us, we had to attend a function in the mess, and they didn't want to come. Probably had to air off their clothes before their flight (!) We had to attend however, and as I entered the Mess, one of the young Officers caught sight of my face. I thought I was smiling, but he was worried for my welfare, thinking I was on the precipice of a breakdown. He offered me a Pimms. He poured it himself ~ a tumblerful with a splash of lemonade, and he felt very pleased to see my normal smile return. So pleased in fact, he offered me another, and so there I was, 2 large Pimms, with 2 teaspoons of lemonade inside me! Now anyone who knows me, knows what I am like with even the whiff of alcohol. I was whooping and laughing ever louder, louder than anyone else there, and even in this state, I knew what I needed to do. I took myself off to the loo to calm down.

I don't know why there were only 2 toilets in the Ladies Room, but it has been the same in all the Messes I've been in, and this one was no different. I lurched through the door, and saw both toilets were occupied, and I couldn't stop laughing. I was holding my sides, and wiping my eyes (I cry when I laugh) and oh, how funny those occupied toilets appeared to be!

I only over-balanced. As I leaned on the vanity units to steady myself, life seemed to go into slow-motion. Oh my!!! There was an almighty crashing as one by one the tiles fell off the walls, followed by the cupboards and basins, leaving the taps and pipes twisted and contorted. And me covered in plaster and grout. And with this plaster and grout still clinging to my eyelashes, 2 women flung open the toilet doors thinking we had been invaded by the Russians and couldn't believe what they saw. What did I do? I ran out of what used to be the Powder Room, and what was now, I suppose, the Plaster Room! I had to report this to the PMC (the Officer in charge of Mess functions)

And who did I find was the PMC? My husband!

And who was he talking to? The chappie in charge of fixtures and fittings!!

It was a good night really, though my in-laws took some convincing that I wasn't a serial alcoholic like their son, and surprise surprise, we got them to the airport in time for the mutually looked-forward-to flight.

I have to own up to something at this point. Something I am not altogether proud of, but nevertheless........

Whenever my family visited these in-laws, I offered £1 to each child who stuck up for me during the visit!!!! I know. I know. But I thought it was good training for them ~ they listened to Granny and Grandpa more intently, AND got their wallets filled. Entrepreneurship. We were all winners. But I could never be sure whether that was the only reason they liked visiting those 2 Grandparents! I must ask them.

XVIII
Holidays

We never agree on holidays. We have had some lovely ones, but usually it's one of us loving it, and the other persevering. The next year that changes, and so it carries on. Funny how we are still together when you come to think of it, but there you are.

Personally, I have things-to-do on holiday. Things like strolling, and taking in the feel of a place. Sipping a coffee at a pavement café, and people-watching. Chatting to locals, visiting markets, and calling in to the odd gallery, all make me extremely happy, followed of course by a great meal in a local restaurant. Back to the Hotel for a glass of wine, and a read of a choice book. Don't like paper-backs, (except if there is no alternative), and then planning my day for tomorrow before I nod off.

Why then, when all this sounds so very perfect, have I married a husband who would rather stick pins in his eyes than spend one of these wonderful days?

His first choice is to get away from civilisation, stretch on a beach, and get through one paper-back after another. When the mood takes him, he may like a cliff top stroll, or worse still, a walk (trek) through the woods. The sort that takes all day!! With binoculars. And a back-pack. And a packed lunch.

Once, when newly married, we went to the Oktoberfest in Southern Germany. Couldn't find a hotel anywhere, and husband had a bad migraine ~ and what do you think? Low and behold, he just happened to have 2 Army camp beds in the boot of the car, along with 2 sleeping bags and a bowl! And where do you think I awoke the following morning? In a field, on a camp bed, and with a cow licking the dew off my sleeping bag! Covered in misty gossamer - YUK. I tripped around with hair drier in my hand looking for a socket to plug it in. Only a fresh-water spring, (so hair-washing out anyway), and I still cannot believe I cleaned my teeth and various private bits in that ice cold water. Not a happy bunny then, and you might think he has got the message by now, but no.

Holidays with 3 children in tow can be a trial, and because we lived in many different places, we tried to introduce them to as many different holidays as we could, which would hopefully furnish them with happy memories.

I know Salzburg was definitely one of my favourites, as was Switzerland, Lichtenstein, and in Italy we loved Venice and Portofino area especially. London being my absolute favourite, but Malta and its history was fantastic. New England in the Autumn ticked all our boxes, especially the clam chowder, which was on offer wherever we went.

Now (despite my name) I have never owned a pair of Jeans in my very long life, not ever. I am more your pearls and handbag battleaxe, and I look ghastly in ultra casual gear. Bottom too big, boobs too big ~ I need to cover up big-style. A trip to New York in Spring then, sounded just the job. My kind of city, shops, theatres, PEOPLE. This was in the 80s, and graffiti was everywhere. Drugs, and gangs were a big problem, and criminality lurked on every corner ~ quite different now, I know, but with 3 children to look after, I clutched on to their collars wherever we went. I cried on a bus heading along Broadway ~ I saw every single tree covered in graffiti and, wet through to my undies during a heavy downpour, a very kind gentleman offered me his brolly. To my everlasting shame I replied "Certainly Not!!!" (I thought it would have drugs tucked inside that he was wanting to get rid of!) I wonder if he still remembers that terribly rude mother with her 3 hands on 3 children's collars??

I tried my first french fries on Staten Island (Yuk!) and our daughter fancied a doughnut from Dunkin Donuts. (Not only do Americans have difficulty speaking English, they cannot spell either) "What flavour?" the American look-down-your-nose lady asked, too disinterested to care. "What choice is there?" said our blonde English daughter. Then came the rhyming off of all the flavours available, each of the 58 delivered with an indecipherable drawl of boredom. Not wanting to upset her, Rachel asked for a banana flavour. "Jesus Christ! We have 58 and you ask for one we haven't got!" Slam went a vanilla doughnut into a bag, not wanting any more conversation with a 7 year old! Customer Service, New York style

Venice suited all 5 of us. We stayed almost on the beach, and Venice, for our eldest son and I, was only a short taxi boat ride away. We were there quite a bit (the others on the beach), and the 2 of us enjoyed the coffees in St Marks Square, the shops, the palaces and markets, and the little back canals with washing hanging out everywhere. Lovely. Our last day was my birthday, and we spent it all together on the beach, with a picnic and bottle of wine. As we left the beach, we saw a crowd gathering, and saw they were looking at enormous sand sculptures ~ of ~ well ~ male genitalia and a pair of boobs. Enormous. And (unknown to us parents) all sculpted by our 3 children!!

We had the usual family conference about where to go on holiday whilst we were in Canada, and I was losing out. Having searched for culture and history in Canada, and found none in our area, I had to concede defeat. The other 4 wanted a fishing holiday, by a lake, in a cabin, by the woods. Oh my lord!! I toyed with the idea of staying at home, but was outvoted, and my husband was despatched to go shopping for fishing rods ~ and daughter wanted a pink one! He searched all the appropriate shops for the pink rod, feeling rather embarrassed at having to walk back to the car with it (?) A happy daughter, and 2 weeks of fishing!! Mmmm.

The cabin was raised off the ground, and a family of raccoons lived underneath. The lake was large, with many twists and turns, and porcupines watched us from up in the trees. Star Wars was big at the time, and daughter and second son were Ewoks, with their own Ewok language, and Ewok sticks, and they played endlessly in the woods.

Fishes were fished for every day (I was the first to catch one)! And husband cooked the catch on the barbeque in the evening ~ at least the ones that hadn't been eaten by the raccoons! The children loved it, even eldest son,~ and soldier husband enjoyed teaching them survival techniques. I, on the other hand hated every single boring minute!! I hated the fish. I hated the raccoons, and the woods, but most of all I hated the ants that enjoyed running over the entire cabin. They were in the pots and pans, cupboards, and, well, everywhere! Sometimes the fat spiders broke the monotony, and they didn't like my screaming at them one little bit. I swear 2 of their spidery legs were used to cover their ears!! Ugh!!

I have always read a lot. I used to like poetry, and I love D H Lawrence, Thomas Hardy, the Brontes, in fact anything (or so I thought!). I read a lot of the Russian Authors at one time ~ I go through different phases with my reading habits ~ Enid Blyton has a lot to answer for, it was she who got me started. On this holiday I took the complete works of Jane Austen. After seeing films, and plays of her work, I thought I would give her a try.

There I lounged on my sun lounger, day after boring day, reading Jane Austen. I shouldn't have bothered! Am I the only one who finds her writing tedious? And tiresome? The tedium of the lifestyle, the shy glances, the search for men with wealth, the tittle-tattle. NO!! Maybe it was the setting I was in, but I never want to read another word of hers again – EVER!.

For the rest of the family, what do you think was the icing on their cake? We booked again to go the next year!!!!!

Now, more or less retired, I have a holiday in my mind, one that is on my bucket list. To travel along the coast of England and Wales, starting at the Scottish border, and travelling clockwise, and ending at the Scottish border on the left of the map. Ha Ha, West I mean!

I would stop off when I wanted to, using hotels and hostelries on the way, and catching up with friends who are scattered all over the place. (and making new ones too).

So, with this lovely holiday firmly embedded, I thought to mention it to my husband, who straight away thought he was included (!) and who told me it would be better to start on the left, and go anti-clockwise. And to use a camper van. So even my day-dreams are being told what to do and where to go!

I, personally, think it would be a cunning plan for me to head off my way, and for him to go his way, and we could meet up on the South Coast. And carry on. He's not keen!

XVIII
Making A Good Impression

I mentioned living in Malta. I loved living there (except perhaps in July or August), and loved its history and the Maltese people who were welcoming, friendly and loyal.

The social life was pretty grand too, and we made many friends, some of whom still are. It seemed easy to socialise when the weather was always good, and we were surrounded by the blue sea and, as the Island is small (about 19 miles long), we felt that we had seen almost every pebble after 2 years. Husband was "Mr Telephones Malta". The person in charge of the crews who installed all the Army, Navy and many Private Rental telephones on the island, and so was a good person to invite to your party when you wanted a phone – they were in very short supply to civilians.

He worked closely with the RAF and Royal Navy, and so we had a bigger circle of acquaintances than usual. The Summer Balls at the RAF were legendary, and the drinks on the Royal Naval ships, were, well, very, very strong!! And we did enjoy them!

Anyway ~ I ramble on. I was going to tell you about my dreadful attempt at making a good impression. And failing.

Now with a small Island like Malta, they were always running out of things. Fruit, cream, cheese, and then onions. When the onions ran out, so did the onion salt, onion rings, onion powder, in fact, anything onion. We heard a shipment was due into the docks, after a lull of about 3 months, and I think the entire population turned out just to watch them unload the onions. There the onions sat in bags on the other side of the fence, with Maltese and Brits just standing there watching them. Motionless (some almost drooling). It was like having a day out.

Joy! My husband's new boss had just arrived from UK, and I wanted to impress him with dinner for 8 at ours. Impress, because we had onions. Even though he must have known nothing about the shortage, I thought 'easy peasy' it's a walk in the park now we have onions, and I started to scan my recipe books. By the way, there was no Jamie Oliver then, and I had to make do with a friend's recipe, she said it never failed. She was wrong. I have been known to cook for many people, and many people have been happy with my food, and as there were only 8 of us I had no qualms as I set off on my culinary quest.

I chose I-can't-remember-what for starters, with Beef Olives (that never failed) for mains, and surprise surprise, Strawberries and Cream. Now that may not sound impressive to you, but we had had a shortage of strawberries too. No one had seen a strawberry for weeks, and then there, on Sliema sea front I spied a man selling them from a van. Lots of them. I bought loads. Hulled and juicy, they sat in the fridge that day in a cut glass dish, covered, and ready to impress. I was very satisfied. Gloating even.

It was hot! No, really hot!! Plus, we needed to keep food and drink cold for the new boss and his wife, and we didn't have enough fridge space. So we filled the bath with cold water and ice and put the selection of mixers, soft drinks and wine in there in plenty of time. New boss man was dying for G and T, and we gladly obliged. Then "Yes thank you, I will have another, but could I have tonic instead of soda?" OMG! The labels had fallen off the bottles in the bath. Everyone had got ~ heaven knows what!

Starter seemed to go ok, but no one knew what wine they were drinking. The picture of the Beef Olives had looked so different from mine, which were like a few floating doo-dahs from the toilet, swimming then disappearing into the stew as they gave up living and collapsed to mush.

I knew at this stage that I could forget any impressing I had wanted to accomplish, so I dolloped the stew onto the plates, and placed a few complete doo-dahs on top, leaving a few precious perfect ones just in case anyone wanted seconds! (like that was ever going to happen) We struggled. We drank lots of unnamed wine. And I don't know how I did it, but I asked if anyone wanted seconds!! I must have whispered it, because my husband obviously didn't hear me, and when I returned with about 4 perfect, saved, doo-dahs, I found he had stacked the plates in a very helpful way. (Big deep breaths).

Right then!! Strawberries and cream! No faffing. Just a straightforward pudding. I uncovered them and could not believe my eyes! Every one of them, every single one was covered in green fungus!! Covered! I didn't cry, in fact I laughed and couldn't stop. I took them to the table and we all laughed. Belly Laughs. And although we didn't know what wine we were drinking, we drank a lot more of it, and as one guest pointed out as he left "Its surprising how you can get used to Rum and Soda!"

The new boss and his wife later became our daughter's god parents, and later still, moved to York, where we too chose to settle.

I've never attempted to make Beef Olives again. In fact I've never been offered them either, but I have a never-fail recipe somewhere if anyone is interested.

XIX
Rotary

I thought the Army was masculine and hierarchical, but it was a tiddler compared to Rotary Club! My husband joined after leaving the Army ~ I suppose wanting the male bonding that was lacking in his second career, and truly, I can understand the need. Up to a point!

The clubs vary in their activities regarding fund raising, and especially with helping the local community, and my husband really enjoyed helping with the community projects. Clearing the local streams and woods, building bird look-outs, and making an area for children to stop and feed the ducks were all things he became involved with. All good so far then, and all done by the males of the species. No females in sight ~ good Lord!, ~ the very thought!! It's here that I must pass on that Rotary Clubs are quite different now, and recruit and invite women into their domain. Not so back in the day!

Off the Rotarians went, once a week, to bask in their maleness, to pat each other on the back for deeds well done, and to plot their next moves. Mostly, all over 50, with some past the 3 score year and 20 mark, and almost all of them firmly fixed in a by-gone era. An era where women bring up their children single-handed, and who send hubby off to work each day with a peck on the cheek and look forward to an afternoon of baking by the Aga. UGH!

Professional men, in professional houses, breeding professional children. Nothing wrong in that of course, but not for me thank you very much. I prefer a mix of friends who either stretch me, or keep me grounded, or both. A group of one type of person and background, seems to me, claustrophobic, especially when they are all of one gender! Some Rotarians were quite nice, but in the club my husband joined they all had one thing in common, and that was to keep women out of their club!! They had an annual vote on whether to accept females, and they donned their flat caps and always voted NO!! At least they did at this particular one in Yorkshire! Good result as far as I was concerned ~ can't for the life of me think why any of us would want to join those dinosaurs.

The Inner Wheel!! This is where Rotarian wives are welcome to run their own version, and lots of them do. Oh My! They meet once a month (women, they think, can only organise to get out of the house on a monthly basis), and owing to the commitment of having to make dinner every night, meet at a hotel for lunch. Just like their men-folk, they have their hierarchy and ranking system ~ President, Treasurer, Secretary, and minions, and even copy the regalia ~ ribbons, badges of rank etc, to denote importance, in case any visitor is in any doubt. Woe betide anyone who speaks up with an idea. If the Lady President hasn't thought of it first ~ no chance!!

I was asked to attend one of their meetings with a view to joining them. Ha! Off to lunch then in the finest hotel the city had to offer, and all dressed up, I was presented to Mrs President. Very limp handshake for someone with a bottom the size of hers. You could have balanced a tea tray on it. I did think I could aspire to this great role one day ~ my backside already veering in the right direction!

I came away with an empty tube of Smarties to fill with 5p pieces and to take back next month. The money was going to feed the poor in Africa!!!!!

I thought long and hard whether to return (at least 3 seconds), and sent my apologies to Mrs Top-Dog, via Mrs Secretary, and gave my collected 5ps to Mrs Treasurer. I know how to go about these things! I wanted to tell them what they should do with the empty Smartie tube ~ it being the correct shape and all ~ but didn't want to let myself down.

They pestered for quite some time, even my husband couldn't understand why I wouldn't commit to it but I held firm. Although I had run Wives Clubs in the Army, (had been president, treasurer and secretary in the past) the clubs were far from hierarchical, and we had many fun times. Because of the fun element, we were well known and all wives were welcomed. Hell, children were catered for too. Rotary is a completely different ball-park, and it wasn't for me.

Every year the Rotarians invited their "Good Lady Wives" to a Summer Ball. Again, very rank-conscious, the President and spouse on the top table with their guests, and the minions finding themselves on the table nearest the drummer! One year, even the band were at their 3 score year and 20, and the drummer fell asleep! Mid drumming!! (Highlight of the evening for me!!) I remember once, a woman on our table said how much she liked my blouse, and how she had admired it the year before!! "Fancy a woman your age remembering what I wore a year ago" I said!

Very occasionally, we wives (Good Ladies) were invited to one of the Rotary weekly meetings, and expected to look decorative. I sat next to another woman with the same humour as myself, and we both sat with napkins stuffed in our mouth so as not to laugh uncontrollably, (and loudly). A Rotarian was sharing his holiday slides with the assembled audience ~ yawn yawn ~ and they were in the Florida Everglades. Unfortunately, whilst not looking at the screen, he was talking about the shot of his wife lounging on a beach, whilst showing a crocodile in the river to the rest of us!!!! Oil of Ulay not working that well then!!

It was at one of these shared meetings when, with a forthcoming Annual Children's Sports Day looming, the committee thought to cash in on what they considered ladies do best. Brew tea!

The gavel banged down on the table, all went quiet, and the committee member took to his feet to give a little talk about how things were progressing. A bumptious little man at best, he put on his most patronising half-smile and addressed himself to the good ladies. "Now ladies ~ I am looking for some volunteers to run the tea tent" he said, "you can bring along your cakes and fancies (?), as usual. The marquee will have been erected by us, and everything ready for when you arrive". (He stopped short of asking us to wear a pretty ribbon in our hair!)

I was livid, but calm too. A quiet seething actually. I worked with a feminist after all, and I wasn't going to let this claptrap carry on. As he sat down, I stood up. "Perhaps the men would care to run the tea tent this year, and the women will erect the marquee" I sat down. He took a while to compose himself ~ I think he must have been on a 'Coping with Challenging Behaviour' course, because he held his corpulent overhang, and took long slow deep breaths to recover. Room silent, and expectant after this terrible outburst from a female! A FEMALE!!

He was brave. I underestimated how brave. As he spoke, he had that terribly smooth sugary slushy patronising voice, and still somehow managing that half-smile of his, he replied. "I think you will find, my dear, that the men will be too busy with the tents". His face seemed blotchy at this point, and I momentarily planned how to mention him having his blood pressure checked. He fumbled to find his seat to sit down, and I stood up. "Oh" I said, "Don't worry, the women will see to all that, and it will give you all time to sort out the tea bags and fancies!" I sat down. He stood up. Bright and breezy now, and rubbing his hands together. He said, "Right, that's sorted then. If the ladies will pop their names on the list and get baking we can all have a very happy tea tent!!"

Tony Benn wouldn't call that democracy. And neither would I!!

The other women there thought I had a death wish, and the men gave my husband a wide berth in the bar, offering their condolences at being lumbered with a wife who had never heard of Stepford!

I didn't care. I went to the damned Sports Day (my sports teacher daughter-in-law said the sports were badly run), and I looked into the tea tent and made a mental note that all the wives were dressed the same, and each with a pretty ribbon in their hair!!

Post Script. The feminist I worked with was my good friend, who was also my boss, and when I asked if I could go on an Assertiveness Training Course, I was surprised at her reaction. Belly laughing for a full 5 minutes!!

XX
Chipping Sodbury (Sodding Chipbury)

Over the last 30 or so years, we have come to love Chipping Sodbury. It IS beautiful, and picturesque, and sitting in the heart of the Cotswolds, are 2 of our friends, Betty and Phil, who some of you may know. That is the BEST part of this lovely biggish village, and I cannot imagine there was ever a visit there that did not start with, comprise of, and end with so much laughter, excellent food, and buckets of wine!! The drive from Yorkshire usually takes us 4 hours, and always full of anticipation we head off down the motorway, looking forward to seeing them (in the affectionately known - "Sodding Chipbury"). Right from the start, you smell Betty's cooking as you park the car, the garlic meeting you before they do, and with wine glass in hand for the next few days, we have the bestest meals anyone could hope for. Their neighbours are forewarned there will be noise, and there is, then comes the doom and gloom as we pack to head back up that same motorway, which by now has no appeal whatsoever!! No appeal, cause we are tired, all-wined-out, sore from laughing, and cannot sit properly on our seats without unzipping, unfastening, unbuttoning our attire, due to excessive over-eating!! We manage to get to Tamworth for our usual stop for coffee, only to find a packed lunch made by Betty on the back seat!!!

When we were both working, I looked forward to the ride

down, it meant I could chat to the man who usually tells me what to do, seeing as we didn't often get the chance for conversations both ways (!). However, on one momentous trip down this didn't happen. I am unable to recall what event caused the anger, but anger there was, on my part, as I packed up the car in complete silence!! Oh I was SOOO angry with HIM, so very angry, as I threw my bags and flowers and choccies for Betty on to the back seat. Not only would I not speak to him, I was actually unable to!! Not one for histrionics as a rule, I would have thought my husband would want to know what had upset me, but well ~ if he didn't know, I wasn't about to tell him!! Childish things like that sped through my brain, as I decided to drive as far as Tamworth, when he would take over. Slam went the doors, and I drove off. Several times he tried to speak, only to be ignored, and I drove in complete silence! Quite fast!!

Signs for Tamworth, (after 2 hours of speed and silence), but I ignored them, and without the Costa Coffee, we continued on this epic journey, ~ still in silence! He slept. How the hell could he sleep??? Blood pressure (mine) quite high at this stage, as I motored faster and faster. I am not proud of this, and good job my police officer son doesn't know about it!! Saw the turn-off we were heading for, and still a tad too fast, I careered around those rural roads like a maniac, only to take a sharp bend and had to swerve to keep on track! 4 hours driving alone, with husband asleep, and he chooses to wake up at that very moment. You couldn't make it up!

A bit on the tetchy side now, he offers to drive, or better still, teach me to, but with only a couple or so miles to go, there was no way I would let him!! No WAY!!

There was Betty, glass in hand, smile on face, and banquet in the oven, opening the door. I literally got out of the car, stormed in, shouting expletives over my shoulder, and a grinning husband caught me up, and said " I think she is more tired than she thought she was!!" All 4 of us, yes, me in included, started the offered wine, laughing off the last 4 hours, and so the outing to Chipping Sodbury continued as usual. Beware the smell of garlic ladies, if you want to continue an argument!!

Betty's cooking is legendary, as is the amount of it, and I have even woken up in the morning to the smell of bacon cooking, then have her knock on the door with a tray of coffee and scones she has just made to tide us over till breakfast. In 10 minutes time!! No use arguing, you have to take it like medicine, cause she wanted to use up some cream!!?? "Oh you will, you will, you willll" in her Irish accent.

You might know that if you say yes to going out for a ride into the Cotswolds, there will be a hamper packed in minutes, complete with cloth, napkins, wine and glasses, and enough food to feed 8. You might just want the hot coffee, but the chocolates, although tempting..... "Oh, you will, you will, you will".

I have known her, as we arrive back from these jaunts, head off quickly into the house, and as we are bringing in the hamper, blankets etc from the car, she is already chopping and peeling the vegetables for the next epic meal!!! "Oh, it's only a little snack", but then we see 3 types of curry on the table!!! Lovingly made, by her, for us, and I have to say, lovingly accepted by us. Betty, you are one true friend, you both are, and our lives would have been missing in fun and friendship without you both. For those reading this, who don't know Betty and Phil ~ get yourselves down to Chipping Sodbury!

We were lucky, and have been invited back, even after all the noise for the next-door neighbour to bear, even after all the washing up, even after their family and friends having to put up with us, we were invited back. And one time we were invited to a birthday party. I can't remember whose big day it was for, it could have been for anyone that day, because there were a lot of people, some who I had never met before, and all drinking wine, or Gin, or both, or more of anything. I was quite, jolly, shall we say, and with glass in hand, was really desperate to go to the loo. The more I laughed, the more the desperation set in, and I am telling you this because it's why I did what I did!

I was so in need of the toilet, I quickly ran in, propped my glass on the washbasin. and literally threw myself onto the toilet. Not having time to look what I was doing, I lifted the seat, but lifted the two together, and with no time to waste, just sat down on the actual porcelain. So far, not too bad, and glad I managed to get there in the nick of time. Walked out of there quite calmly, well, I thought so, and joined a group to chat to. We got quite animated, and the chappie next to me, put his arm around my waist (I thought it weird too), and then he started to fumble around the area that at that time was where my waist was, and now isn't. Seemed to go on for a bit, this fumbling, then someone else noticed the rather large lump, protruding from under my clothes! Oh my goodness!! Seems that when I sat on the actual porcelain toilet, I acquired the hanging Blue Loo thingy, which had got caught up in my knickers, and which was firmly in place for all to feel. And they did!! And with blue-stained undies, I headed for the food!!

Betty and Phil have followed us on our postings and moving for the last 30 plus years, and after meeting them in Bristol, we moved to Harrogate, Ripon, Devon, and York. All good places for fun weekends. First time to Harrogate they (BETTY) misread our map, and turning off in Leeds when they thought they were in Harrogate was their first mistake! They were due at about 10pm, but by 2am had not shown up. A phone call told us they were close by, but lost, so John headed out to find them. They were not where they thought, but had found ME by this time, and now John was missing!! (no mobiles in those days). Probably got to bed by about 4am, after a few Harvey Wallbangers. "Oh Betty, you will, you will, you will".

Those Wallbangers became a feature, and when they came North to Harrogate again for the Army November 11th weekend, we were happily partaking of a few the night before we were to attend the Church Service of Remembrance. Betty is Catholic, but the Service was C of E. I am neither, but like to attend as an act of remembrance.

She had had more than she usually had of the Wallbangers the night before, and says the only time she ever felt the bed spinning around, was that night. I believed her. The morning after, we found ourselves at the front of the church, and sat down. Betty straight away, I thought, put her head down, and began to pray, like I have seen them do in churches, so I left her to it. Her head had been thumping over breakfast, as had mine, and I sat beside her as she prayed. It is here that Betty and I have different versions of the next few minutes. I say she told me she wasn't praying, but was trying to stop herself from being sick! SHE says she was praying, and I was feeling ill. Whichever version you feel like believing, think what you like my friends!!! Ha ha!

My lovely friend even helped in our shop in York a couple of times, and although she had trouble seeing over the top of the till area, managed remarkably well (for her height). She used her, "you will, you will, you will" method of selling, and off the customers went with more candles than they came in for, but with smiles on their faces.

Then came the recession, and the shop went downhill, until it came to stand-still and we were forced to close. We lost the shop, we lost our house, and we lost our car. Luckily, we kept our friends, and what on earth do you think our good friends from Chipping Sodbury did??? They gave us their second car!!!! Still to this day I cannot believe they did that. Not only that, but when we went to collect it, Phil had filled it up with petrol!!!

Betty and Phil from Chipping Sodbury ~ we can never repay you, and we will be forever grateful to you both, so hurry up, pack that bag, and come and see us soon, we are suffering from C S withdrawal, and could do with sharing a couple of Woolacombe Horlicks's!! - Amarula to those not in the know .... "you will, you will, you will".

XXI
Guest House Devon

I sometimes have a bright idea. Or is it a cunning plan? We have moved so much in our married life, and I never seem able to to put down roots. When husband left the Army, I missed, (and still do) him coming home and saying "Guess where we are going next?" My feet itch to move on, and after 9 YEARS (longest ever stay anywhere before) living in Ripon, we put our lovely Haven Cottage up for sale.

Didn't take long to sell, but one snowy afternoon in February, I was at work, and John was to show a couple around. Sniffy couple really, with long noses to look down at you from a superior height. First they wanted to go outside to see the garden (under snow?), and to kick the drainpipes(?) and presumably to check out the roof. Satisfied, my other half then started the grand tour inside. I came home whilst they were upstairs, and Oh my Lord!!! WHAT a smell!!! Ugh!! I thought I didn't want THEM to live in our house, and I held my nose as I hung up my coat. Poor John was looking pale, with a raised-eye-look, and a finger under his nose to halt the smell. We certainly did not give them any indication we were about to accept an offer from them ~ not a chance!

Out they were ushered rather quickly, and the two of us choked loudly as we closed the door. Then we saw the newly-shampooed carpet!!! Trails and trails of dog poo mixed with melting snow!! Y-U-K!! (and firmly embedded in the new sheepskin rug)!! Must have picked up the poo from outside in the snow, so hubby now ranting about hounds, and their owners, and the deterioration of life as we know it!! We don't do dogs. Have never had them ~ I am even known as Cruella de Ville ~ so obviously poo from a canine is not a smell we could ever get used to. And I can think of nothing so undignified than following a dog with a plastic bag to scoop up a smelly sausage. Filling the carpet shampooer again though, I gave in to a larger-than life belly laugh!! THEY must have thought our house was evil-smelling and couldn't wait to get out, and WE thought they were a foul couple ankle-deep in dog poo at home and we couldn't wait to kick them out!!

Husband didn't laugh. He was busy setting up an air rifle to point at the gate, preparing to wait for the 4-legged creature with a death wish and diarrhoea, for as long as it took!!

We sold a fresh clean house, and 2 Pickford lorries went in convoy to Woolacombe, in Devon, where we had bought a Guest House by the sea.

Arriving there at the start of the school summer holidays wasn't our finest moment! (13 bedrooms and a bar to look after, and hot hot hot). Plus, the 2 lorry-loads of furniture were everywhere, including dining room, halls, kitchen, our flat, and we had 14 guests staying!! The outgoing owners came by to say hello, and to remind us that we had 12 for dinner that very night! There was not a pan that was useable and the fridges were rusty and filthy, and a health hazard.

We both lost 2 stone in 5 weeks. I was too tired to eat and too tired to talk! We were up at 6.30, cooking and serving breakfasts, bed-changing, cleaning, change-overs, and cooking dinners. My other half in the bar, and me doing the laundry until gone 1am. 7 days a week. Just the 2 of us.

We had 2 new, enormous fridges delivered which we later called the twin towers, and thank goodness for our young niece, who came from Bolton to help us. The 3 of us managed somehow, but I would not recommend it to an enemy.

The morning eggs were the worst. It's surprising how everyone has a different idea of "a lightly boiled egg". And how the guests can change their fickle "I'm On Holiday" minds!! They loved asking for scrambled, and when served, were sure they asked for poached. They loved that one!! John was a shade of puce most mornings, but hey...somehow we coped. We replaced kitchen equipment, bought new bedding, decorated, stopped the evening meal, and closed the bar. And we made a living with just bed and breakfast for 2 years. Still hard work, but much more manageable.

Surfers came from London in the Autumn, which is when I realised we lived by the sea!! Hadn't surfaced since we moved in, and outside had been a beautiful 3 mile stretch of clean, clean beach, and the Atlantic Ocean.

Our daughter rang me on her way home from work in York one dark November night, complaining that she hated her job at the bank. Another cunning plan was forming, and I asked her what she thought about working with us if we sold the Guest House, and bought a shop. Anywhere! Impulsive as me, we were both in agreement, and after the call it took me a whole 10 minutes to do some sums. By the time she got home I had my plan ~ the only person to convince now was my other half!! After 15 minutes we were looking for Commercial Estate Agents! Impulsive? Why not? 6 months later we were on the move to our Candle Shop in York!!

I am such a liar! When the Guest House was advertised,

we had 2 weeks with potential buyers queueing up to view, sometimes 5 or 6 a day. I saw them in at the front door, oh how lovely I made it all sound and as the doorbell rang with more buyers, I handed them over to my husband who did the same as me, and showed them out of the back door! A continuous stream. We had lots of offers, and it went to tender, we chose carefully, and it SOLD.

The poor sods (sorry, new owners), gratefully took it off our hands. And we were MORE than grateful to them!!

Post Script.
Queueing in the post office to send our change of address cards, a lady caught my arm and said how sorry she was we were leaving, just as she had got to know us! I had never seen her before. Must have been peering from behind her net curtains in that insular, curtain-twitching village that is Woolacombe. A village where you need to be a resident for 105 years to be accepted ~ or maybe that is the whole of Devon? I will never know, I don't care enough to find out!

XXII
Women's Institute

Even now, I am not opposed to the WI. I know the clubs vary in their activities, and I know lots of women get a lot out of them ~ but not me!

The thought of those middle-aged Yorkshire women baring their bits for charity is not my idea of feminism, and yet they think it is, just because they can if they want to. Fair point. But how come, to sell a calendar for charity in the 21st century, they feel they have to undress? And with that naughty naughty look in their eyes, as they don't go the full hog, but hide behind their fairy cakes in case someone might just see something.

However, these are my own thoughts. Personally, I prefer to keep my wrinkles to myself and under wraps ~ tucked away where prying eyes and sarcastic thoughts cannot reach! MY wrinkles! MY bits! MY folds of skin! (I usually wear Winceyette nighties from the frill under my chin, to the frill around my feet ~ how's THAT for feminism!!) Just because I can!!

Living in Woolacombe was quite a lonely existence. Running a busy Guest House in Summer didn't leave any time or energy for socialising, but come November it was very quiet. Winter was for decorating and making changes, and the neighbours were all doing the same. As I hadn't lived in Woolacombe for more than 100 years, locals crossed the street rather than chat. Or nod. Or look, even. Family in London, and in Sheffield were a long way away, and it was a 34 mile round trip to even go to Tesco. Not surprising that when I did go to shop, I harangued the poor shop assistants into talking to me whether they wanted to or not. And usually they didn't!

I saw an advert in a shop window for new members for the local WI, and as it was the Christmas meeting, I went along to the Church Hall thinking I might meet more people in a Christmassy atmosphere ~ a 'special'. I think by 'special', I envisaged wine!

It was like walking into Miss Havershams' attic! Cobwebs and dust everywhere, and a smell of rotting wood. The Christmas tree was slightly askew due to the slope of the floor, and not all lights were working. Well, most really. Lots of ladies there (women), and all averted their eyes as I walked in, and who all of a sudden found lots-to-do, and tea-to-make!! I plonked down at one of the tables and made the lady next to me talk to me. My cup of tea arrived. I don't drink tea ~ I hate the stuff, but I offered to make myself a coffee if they could point me in the direction of the kitchen. Nothing forthcoming ~ I had obviously asked a heinous question ~ and the thoughts of the possible wine thing were quickly disappearing.

I was asked if I had brought a FOM (flower of the month). What? Seemingly, at every meeting you are expected to bring a flower from the garden, and put it in a pot on the dusty mantelpiece, and everyone places a 5p piece on the one they like the best. This way they collect the money for charity, and on this special Christmas meeting they made ~ oh, about £1.95!! Same went for the home made Christmas cards.

After this hilarity, it was time to start the meeting, and all WI meetings are started by singing Jerusalem. The untuned and extremely dusty piano had the kiss of life, and they all set forth. I cannot sing, am not churchy, and if I don't believe what I am singing, I just stop. My new best friend said I could bring a song-sheet next time if I didn't know the words!! I have lost count of the many, many times I have found myself in church, mouth tightly shut (for once) gazing at my feet and wondering how long before I could leave! Jerusalem was not about to change me!!

Minutes of meetings long since dead and buried were gone through with accurate precision. The recent trip to the Carol Concert in Exeter Cathedral was dissected, with all stops for toilets discussed, and conversations they had had along the way recounted for us all to hear. The suitability or not of the disabled toilets in the tea shop was analysed, and apparently, a good time was had by all!

We had a speaker. A plummy woman with a cut-glass accent who had come all the way from Godalming to share her recipes and tips for hectic housewives at Christmas. We were given copies of her recipes to treasure, "Now then ladies" she said, "We all know what it's like to make a cake, and with no time to fill it. There it sits in the pantry, (come on now) until that cake needs stuffing" (!) Hey presto ~ she had the very cake in front of her!! She proceeded to whip the cream, and mix in some Nutella, and filled the bare cake to within an inch of it's life! We could find the recipe in the leaflet!!!!! Why had I never thought of this ingenious plan?? If I had made a cake there is no way it would sit in a pantry ~ no more than 10 minutes that is!

Quickly losing the will to live, and remembering I had toenails to cut, I escaped as soon as I could. My new best friend caught my arm and offered to pick me up for the next meeting (heaven forbid), but I told her I was going to London that week. She rang me again ~ to arrange the next month, but not such a coward this time, I told her WI was not for me. I never saw her again!

Reading the local Devon newspaper, later, I was attracted to the WI 2- page spread that was in every month. All village Women's Institute shenanigans from around the whole of Devon were reported on, thread to needle. I had missed Darning for Beginners in March! Damn!!

XXIII
London

I just LOVE London!!! I love the noise, I love the traffic, I love the underground, and best of all I love the shops! When the East Line train arrives at Kings Cross my spirits rise in a way that they never do anywhere else, and I have a real feeling of belonging. I know, you have probably stopped reading now, and tut-tutted at this slightly deranged woman banging on about a smelly city, but I truly believe it is my "spirit city". I feel slightly the same about Venice, which I know is a bit like Marmite ~ you either love Venice or hate it ~ my husband being on the hate-ish scale! I love going behind the facade and seeing the buildings, with washing hanging out on balconies, and the little bridges joining people across the water. My husband just sees the banana peel on the water, but I see the romance of it all. And the ice cream!! And the coffee!! And the pizza!! Back to London!!

My idea of a good walk is along Regent Street, and popping in to Bond Street, whereas my husband's idea of a good walk is negotiating cliff paths, or woods, or moors and Dales. HIS "spirit place" being the Malvern Hills. Lots of them, and with binoculars, and walking boots, and compass. Oh, and a bottle of water!! And Kendal Mint Cake!! My idea of hell, and I wonder how we have been married for 55 years. In answer to that one, it's probably because we spend so much time apart!!

He is sporty, and competitive, and I am not. He likes odd music. I like my choices only. I love the theatre, ballet and opera, he hates them. He reads silly books (in my view) like Terry Pratchett, and I like books on psychology, and PEOPLE. Good job we like each other then, warts and all!!

Back to London ~ sorry, I get easily distracted! But not when I am in Liberty. Oh how I love that store, have you seen the staircase, and the landings? I always enter through the florist area ~ where I have told my family I would like my ashes to be buried!!!! Yes, I have told them! I have looked at the floor, and they have black and white tiles, so just easing one up would not be too much of a problem, and I could rest easy every day smelling all those beautiful flowers, and still be in London. The look of astonishment on their faces says it all really, but we shall see. An alternative to Liberty florist shop-under-the-tiles-scenario, is to scatter them on the streets~ you know ~ like in that prisoner of war film where they dug tunnels, then put the soil in their trousers to scatter as they walked along, and no one notices as bit by bit they rid themselves of the dirty dirt. It could work!!

My all-time favourite poem is UPON WESTMINSTER BRIDGE, and my arty son drew me a picture of the bridge which I love, and wrote the poem in the corner. That poem is engraved on a plaque at the London Eye. If you want to, look it up, enjoy it, it says it all, and if you don't, well that's ok too.

In the meantime, and because I am not being turned into ashes for another 50 years, I continue to be a volunteer advocate, and enjoy that almost as much as anything! Not as much as enjoying my family, ~ as long as they don't want me to go for walks into the "green stuff" (countryside!).

XXIV
Sport

I feel I am about to gripe, well, actually, I know I am, so apologies to anyone it will offend. The problem is, I know that hate is a strong word, and yet every time I see any sport, hear any sport, or anyone talks to me about it, every hair on my body stands on end, and I just want to bellow STOP IT!!! Is that hate? Probably.

I suppose I haven't the slightest desire to beat anyone at anything ~ I don't want to win anything, and I certainly don't want to watch anyone else doing any winning or losing. Oh my, the faces on those footballers when they score a goal says it all, and WHAT a waste of champagne at the Formula 1 winners podium. What a grumbling old woman I have turned into, but my thoughts on this are due to the amount of sport I have endured during my long marriage, and the amount of sport my husband has played or supported especially during his time with the Army.

Hours and hours listening about his training regime, hours of watching him carry out the training, and being informed thread to needle how he can improve half an inch on his javelin throw. Or discus throw. And watching him practice, again and again. Then comes the Athletic Match ~ and he wins his throwing matches, but the drawback afterwards, and just as I am about to leave for home, is the discussion about everyone else's throws! STOP IT!! Please. It is here I own up to MY delight in those championships. I look as though I fully support the whole thing, smile on face, sitting with other bored wives, and clapping my hands at the correct time. But with my sports bag always within reach. My sports bag is a basket that holds 3 bottles of wine, and 6 glasses. Please don't knock it, it got me through so many track and field events, along with the other bored wives, and now has pride of place on the fireside, empty of wine, but with a peace lily plant thriving inside it. Job done!

Just as you thought I had finished groaning, that same husband took up orienteering and thought I would love to take our 3 young children to watch him. The youngest being 18 months old. Off we set to go to the woods, picnic in car, on our way to an adventure running through trees. Well, watching others run through trees. One problem! It poured with rain! All afternoon. All 4 hours! 3 young children in their car seats, bored, crotchety, and wanting to be anywhere else. And no sign or a glimpse of daddy. The wet-through runners came back in varying stages of decay, and just as we thought of home, those wet-through decaying individuals spent another hour discussing everyone else's experiences with the terrain!!! A very quiet ride home in the car!

Happy to report though, that I was unable to watch the shooting matches he seemed to win a lot of, but then still had the breakdown of most of the bullets fired, and the targets they hit. But now I am thankful I don't hear too much about the bowls that he joins other like-minded old men to play (but only when his knees don't let him down). Too much throwing in the past I reckon! Have just remembered one good thing about the javelin. It's now used as a clothes prop.

A proper use for it at last!

I need to stop the moaning, and relate that I have a wonderful daughter in law who is head of PE at a secondary school, and her daughter, my gorgeous granddaughter, is also a PE teacher. My son came out of University as a PE teacher, but is now in the Police Force. Where did I go wrong?

As for me, well I don't need a trophy for watching ballet or opera, or the Nation interviewing me for the latest update on my training schedule. The recognition I get from family and friends is all I need, plus the odd belly laugh with Prosecco in hand, when a footballer fails to get the latest sports car. Or a footballer's wife is taken to court for talking to a friend. Then - I'm a happy bunny.

All that is, except for one thing. PLEASE BBC 1 AND 2 please stop putting sport on daily from 9 am right through to 11.45 pm mainly during the summer, and wiping away all other programmes that I want to watch! Must be SOMEONE who agrees with me? Thank you, and enough about sport, I need a break!!

XXV
Team Work

Team work. I have always worked as a member of a team, and I must say, I am very used to it. Myself and my husband are a team, my family are a team, and the people I have worked with have all been parts of teams. Sounds a bit sickly ~ (I can almost hear you saying Y-U-K!!) ~ and you can be forgiven for that, except I love the feeling of everyone helping each other.

Back in the day when I worked for Social Services, myself and another team member were transferred to a different office in a nearby town. Still working for an Older Persons Unit, we thought the set-up would be the same as the one we had left. Wrong!! We were used to chatting together, to make coffee for each other, and the best bit of all, was when we came back from a stressful visit, and found a friendly face who put the kettle on. Support being there as and when needed. Not so in this new office. No one welcomed us, no one spoke, and no one seemed to speak each other. Heads down, it was work-work-work!! We sorted the new little office which the two of us shared, put our bits and pieces in place, and sat looking at each other for a couple of days. The others in a larger office got on with their worky things, not looking up when we breezed in, and probably thinking we were from the devil himself judging by their expressions!!

So ~ one lunchtime my colleague went to the toy shop and bought some plastic traffic cones that kiddies play with. Lots of them. I bought some ground coffee and fairy cakes, and we set out the double row of cones from their doorway, down the corridor to our office, in such a way, that they couldn't miss the road to our office without climbing over them. There they stood, in our doorway, with surprised faces wondering what had just happened, and we met them with filtered coffee and cakes, and most importantly got to know them!!! Job done. Only one thing though. The cleaners had to pass, the admin staff had to pass, and the bosses had to pass, all on their way out, so we even got to know all of them too!!! PS ~ fairy cakes ran out all too soon!!

A great success, 'cause at Christmas we were all so much part of a team, that we got the tree up, decorated it whilst listening to the carols on the radio, and arranged our small gifts under it. Ahh, happy days with the group of people who became our friends and who all came to stay at our guest house when my husband and I moved to Devon.

I wonder if the person who stumbled across the coffee

bean in years gone by, would ever have thought it would be responsible for teams being built??

XXVI
Navigation

I have a wire in my brain that doesn't seem to be connected like other peoples. It's the bit that plays a big part in my never quite knowing where I am. You might laugh, especially as I am a volunteer advocate now, and the least you might expect, is my knowing my whereabouts, but that's the way I am.

The problem of this malfunction has been known to my family and myself for a long period of time, and in some part I blame Malta! I learned to drive whilst living there, and the Maltese drive on the side of the road that's in the shade. Or at least they used to. From there we lived in Birmingham, and I lived in fear approaching Spaghetti Junction, but soon battled the elements, and fought my way like everyone else. No wonder, I had plenty of practice ~ I was always on the wrong road!

I remember driving my 3 children to see a HUGE statue in Germany, one that could be seen on top of a hill, from miles around. Probably the biggest statue I had ever seen ~ but we only saw it from the car, one after another of my off-spring squealing and laughing as they spied it from one side of the car, then the other! Then through the rear window – and even through the sunshine roof! Not knowing which road to drive on, I did a tour of West Germany, and returned home, in the hope their dad would take us at some point. He did! (I apologise to my feminist friends!!). One mention of "Herman's Denkmal" reduces some of us to curled up laughter, gasping for breath with painful stomachs and others to feelings of awful gibbering uncertainty! No doubt you can guess who that is.

Now living in York, and volunteering as an Advocate I know my limitations on getting around, ~ especially having to do that on time. So, I took myself to WH Smith, and bought a street map. Good thinking, and the best thing I have done since we came here.. Well, not THE best, but it's helped. I own up to one roundabout giving me grief. The one off the A64, the one where Grimston Bar comes off. The one road I want, but until recently have chosen every other, sometimes the ones I have chosen taking me to the Designer Outlet!! I always eventually get to where I want to be, and at this point, would like to reassure everyone, that I never put this mistaken mileage on my expenses form!!! Oh, and a tip for any of you in the same position, ~ I made that roundabout easier to navigate, by turning the map upside down!

Why oh why do the map makers insist on having the motorways AND rivers coloured blue?? Roads are red or yellow on maps, and small roads white, and I can navigate them quite easily, but the colour blue leaps out at me as I try to get on the M1,only to find I need a canoe! I might have to bring myself up-to-date and use Sat Nav, but something stops me. I think it's because I don't like being told what to do. When the car informs me I need to change gear, I say out loud "I will if I want to!"

My husband is great with maps, and can read them like reading a book ~ for pleasure. Weird. He looks where the sun is, and knows East from West, that sort of thing, whereas I have a problem finding my way to the ladies in Marks and Spencer, and they are signposted ~ with arrows!

I remember driving myself and 7 year old daughter from UK to Germany. I knew the way, we had done it several times, and we took the cross channel ferry from Hull to Rotterdam. Got to Hull and onto the ferry. We had a cabin booked, but knew we had to be off the ferry at 6 am the following morning. All good so far then you may think. Woke early, and got a quick shower, make-up applied, hair done, and fully dressed, now was the time to get my daughter up. Problem. I just could not raise her, no matter how I tried, she was FAST asleep. It was then I noticed the clock ~ it was 3 am!! Back to bed fully clothed then.

Yes, made it off the ferry by 6 am, straight into the thickest pea soup fog I had ever seen. The signs over the 8 lane roads leading to various motorways could not be seen in that fog, and I got on the wrong one, and ended up round the back street of Rotterdam still foggy, surrounded by cyclists intent on getting to work as quickly as possible. Haha, daughter sitting in the back telling me not to worry (?). Thank goodness for a kind gentleman who pointed (vaguely) towards the road to Germany, and lo and behold ~ we actually got there!! Without a map, because the blue motorways were outnumbered by the canals!! Probably why I am grey haired now, and he will never know how he helped a helpless woman, who still suffers with navigation, (or should I say from lack of it!). My daughter on the other hand never gets lost with her sat nav telling her "what to do".

So, if you see a lighthouse that's lost, whose light is on but there is no one in, please point it in the right direction ~ it might not go where you tell it to go, they tend to be a bit stroppy!

XXVII
The Middle, Or Maybe Past It!

Well, thank you for getting this far through my ramblings, but don't feel bad if you didn't. You will not be alone, and you can always use the book for something else. Like lighting the fire in these austerity months we are living through just now! Or to prop up a wobbly table leg, or even to just tear the pages up in a fit of rage for the wasted time spent on reading drivel. I will not mind one bit.

Thought to explain the few tales that are next in the marathon of your read. After retirement, I became a Volunteer Advocate in York, where I tried my hardest over the last 11 years to help anyone over the age of 50, to help solve their problems ~ or whatever they are not coping with. I have loved every moment of doing this, have met many, many lovely people, and been helped myself by the extremely helpful staff in the office. I promise to learn how to copy and paste ....eventually!

Whilst being an Advocate, I wrote several blogs for our website, titled Vocal Volunteer. Short blasts of a range of topics, and if you don't like them, well, nothing I can do about that now, except to apologise. With a promise that I will learn one day how to navigate a map, and maybe, just maybe to have a chat about sport! OK then, but don't hold your breath ~ those promises may be a long time coming!

Deep breath then....!

XXVIII
Mobiles

Have been watching how people seem to be so pre-occupied with their mobiles that they are oblivious to what is going on around them.

Sitting on the bus; there they are, head down, not taking notice of anything or anyone, and I need to ask ~JUST WHAT ARE THEY LOOKING AT? Is it a game, is it a text, is it photos, or is it just switching off from life? Worryingly, mums with children in pushchairs, can also be seen to do the "switching off thing", which always surprises me, because with 3 children, and 7 grandchildren, I just know for sure that there is so much to see and to talk to children about during a bus ride! Once, (seems like a hundred years ago), I had a rare day on my own when we lived in Birmingham. A day without children, and with the shops waiting for me in their masses, I went into the city on the bus. I enjoyed heading upstairs, a rare treat, 'cause I usually had children and a pushchair to contend with, but there I sat at the front of the top deck, looking like a normal person! We were approaching the fire station, when a fire engine roared out of the station, with blue lights flashing, and the siren going full blast. The mother in me pointed, and said in very loud voice, "look everyone, a fire engine!!!" Yes, the passengers laughed at me!!

I felt a bit daft!!!

My husband on the other hand, was on the bus the other day (I always kidnap the car), when a woman sitting behind him carried on a very loud conversation with a friend on her mobile. A conversation about their mutual friend who had just found out she was pregnant, and whose name the woman on the bus talked about loudly, but told her friend not to tell anyone else! My husband had had enough, and turned around to tell the woman, "too late for that, the whole bus knows now!!!" Yes, passengers laughed with him.

He felt a bit satisfied!!!

So, if you are like me, and notice what is going on around you, and who travels through life without a nose constantly in the mobile, perhaps becoming a volunteer may be for you! You will have noticed there are people out there, through possibly no fault of their own, and for many many reasons, might just be grateful for someone like us to take notice, and for that someone to offer them help with a problem they cannot, at that moment, cope with alone.

I love it when the outcome is good, and I feel satisfied I have done my best when occasionally the outcome has not gone so smoothly. I keep my mobile fully charged, and with me most of the time, but my nose is firmly pointing ahead.

You might say I sound a bit smug!!! - Sorry!!!

XXIX
Television

I watch some rubbish on television. I do. I have my favourite programmes of course, but occasionally the rubbish creeps in, and an hour of my life has gone, never to return. Of course, when I say "rubbish", I know a host of people would be offended if I named these programmes, they are inevitably someone else's favourites! That's the way it goes, and we can't please everyone all the time, can we?

MY go-to programmes usually suit me due to the enjoyment I get from people-watching. I just love it! Love Question Time, 'cause those politicians are so good at avoiding the question asked, then their body language says it all. Same with Daily Politics. Some of them haven't mastered the art of squirming have they, and oh how I love to see a good interviewer hit the target with a probing question! At this point you are thinking how very nasty of me to find entertainment in someone else's downfall, ~ and I have to say, I would be thinking the same, but for me, I like to hone my skills in the people-watching department. It stands me in good stead when I am up against officialdom and I am doing my best to help a client or two. That language of the body is a dead giveaway!!

I own up to watching Escape to the Country!!! Please don't ask me why, 'cause I would never in a hundred years want to live in the country!! I would not even be paid to do it! The moors are a frightening place, with NOTHING to interest me, and woods too frighten the life out of me ~ especially just as it's getting dark! Fields are full of animals that don't want you there, and should you wish to have a picnic, and actually SIT, then surely a million insects will meet their demise!! Especially in my case, my rear end possibly covering the whole of the rug!

No, it's not the countryside that interests me on this programme, it's the house-hunters. A wonderful opportunity for people-watching, as they say they want to "downsize" but well, not really~'cause "these rooms are small!" Then they shuffle about as they are taken to a type of house they said they didn't want, like the ones who hate beams, but are shown a home with so many beams that the rooms look like cells. "Is this too small for you?" the presenter says, as they stand in a loft conversion, backs against the wall, and necks pushed forward 'cause they can't stand up straight. "No, I think this is a good size" they say, lying!! Oh, rich pickings for the likes of me, who revels in the body-language on offer.

I think the BBC are missing a chance here, I would pay good money to see Escape FROM the Country!! My idea of a good walk is up and down Regent Street, with the occasional trot into Bond Street, and whilst I think of it,~ why do they put residential homes tucked away in the country, or at the back of trading estates? For me, I would love to be in one on a High Street, enjoying the comings and goings of the town through a window, with a good flat meander into the shops when I felt like it.

And so, as I said I love the people-watching, and the body-language, and to see a clients face light up with relief when a problem is solved is good enough for me. (I love a happy ending!) And if, like me, you love helping, why not join our team,~ but PLEASE don't watch my body, ~ it's not a pretty sight!!!

XXX
Ageism

There are all sorts of isms that people get irate about aren't there, and by golly, irate IS how they get, myself included sometimes. In my earlier, younger, ~ ok then MUCH younger days, it was feminism. Heaven forbid I would burn my bra like some well known women were doing ~ not really my thing ~ but I did, and still do, dislike the thought that men were in certain boxes, and women were in theirs. I am all for equality if possible, and as a woman am not minded to be thought of as a servant at home.

I would add to that, and state that if both parties were happy with this, who should object? Certainly not me, I always wanted everyone to be happy with their life, and as I look back to the 50s, and then 60s when I got married, the 2 parties (in the main) followed the pattern of the man working, and the wife being at home bringing up the children. You notice I don't mention her "working" at home ~ as a young wife when anyone asked what your job was, most replies were "I'm just a housewife"! Thank goodness the perception has shifted, and I hope by now that as an oldie, I appreciate the difference.

To me, the ism in feminism means having choices, and I am all for that! One of my mantras over the years when anyone asked me what I did, was "I'm an independent woman in the prime of my life"!! Well,~ my other mantra was "Don't you just love wine?" Both of them being copied by my daughter who is a working mother with children. I even started a what's app group titled Independent Women in the Prime of our Lives, and we have a group chat which is sometimes hilarious.

Two of them have been friends of mine for years when we were Army Wives and who fought tooth and nail for the Army to use our correct names. All wives used to be referred to as WO, (wife-of) husband's name rank and number. When in an Army hospital, visiting an Army doctor, or seeing an Army dentist, we were all down as WO blahh blahh. Sons were SO and daughters were DO. It took years of campaigning but we got there in the end, and we all received a memo from on high (MOD) that all wives and families of serving personnel were to be referred to by their correct names from that date. Success!! I have that very memo, framed, and it used to hang in the downstairs toilet ~ a fitting place I thought!

And so now I am a Volunteer Advocate and am able to voice my thoughts and feelings, which I can do at any time, ~ at the same time taking my clients thoughts and feelings and projecting them to the appropriate recipient on their behalf. A role which I love, and so I was appalled recently at a phone call I had the other day.

I had kept a personal appointment, an hour away from my home, and was 20 minutes early. No one there, door locked, car park empty and not a soul in sight. Oh dear. An hour later, and still could not get into the building, and still no one to be seen. What to do? Could not telephone, as all calls had to go through head office, and they are only avail on Mon-Fri ~ this was on a Saturday. Headed home, and rang head office early Monday morning.

Was quite calm, expecting a mistake was made, and lets face it, we have all made those, but the man I spoke to informed me, in a voice I have got used to as I get older (condescending and sugary-sweet) that the place WAS open on that Saturday, but that I must have been confused as there are a lot of office buildings around that all look the same!! My reply, I have to say, was via the steam coming off me and went something like "I may be 75 but I have been twice before to that office, and the 6ft letters on the wall tell me it is the correct office, and if they checked the CCTV they would see a 75 year old trying for an hour to get in"!!! And he was then blaming my "confusion" as their excuse for a mistake~that HE had made~my original appointment for a day when they never open on Saturdays anyway. Apologies from him on the company's behalf (calls are monitored) but a feeling that ageism has caught me up, except that I am going to get the better of him, re-educate him, and if I can't, I know some brilliant friends on a WhatsApp group who will!

Oh, and if I get a letter of apology, I may just frame it, and hang it in the spare toilet!

XXXI
Names

Are you one of those people who always remembers names? Well, I am not, and it annoys me I am not, and there doesn't seem to be anything I can do about it. I have tried various strategies that have been recommended to me, strategies that other people appear to find useful, but apart from actually writing someone's name on a sticky note and slapping it onto their chest, nothing has worked!

It really isn't socially acceptable is it, to be nattering away animatedly, glass of wine in hand, and looking like a rabbit in the headlights when another person joins your group in an effort to make contact. I can look extremely gormless with little effort at the best of times, but this scenario throws me completely, because I just know introductions are expected! And worryingly, I just KNOW I am unable to do the honours, not even if I were to gabble for an hour, hoping the name will leap into my vacant memory box!! (It never does).

I've tried to feign a coughing fit, have made fun of the wine-slurping numbing my lips, and the best yet, have actually asked them to spell their name so I can get the hang of an introduction. Mortifying!! My humour usually gets me out of the tightest of corners. I didn't even flinch when a visiting Colonel came to dinner, and as I'd cleaned the bathroom to within an inch of it's life, thought to hang a large label on the towel rail to deter any of my 3 children from using the clean towels. The label read ~ "KEEP YOUR MUCKY PAWS OFF THESE TOWELS!!" Unfortunately, my lack of memory let me down, and I forgot to remove the label, and, yes, he went to the bathroom!!!!! The Colonel certainly remembered MY name ~ he repeated it on several occasions, and always with a guffaw that stays with me now.

I love the training sessions at the office though. Great!! Always a sticky label for name, and with a good pen to really etch it into that lovely, white, gleaming badge, that automatically lets everyone know who you are!! Thoughtful!!! I think the folks in the office should wear one at all times, ~ well ~ for when I visit at least! I was in there the other day, when in came the lovely Dan, who grinningly said hello, only for me to say "Ah, hello Fred!"!!! WHERE did that name come from??? I have no idea. And I apologise!!

I must think of a coping mechanism for when I visit clients. I already swot up their name before I meet them, and I am trying my hardest not to forget their name whilst I am with them, and so far, not too bad. Somehow, I find myself asking for their patience ~ at times gently repeating the mantra, "I am not too good with names ~ but I never forget faces".

I should use that same mantra on my grandchildren. Their names often mix me up, there are two brothers whose names start with O, and a brother and a sister whose names start with A. Their parents have a lot to answer for, I mix them up all the time! Thank goodness for the other two, who have an A and an M. Never mix THEM up.

Oh well, roll on older age, when I will have the best excuse going!! And I will hope for an advocate who might just have a brain cell left in their memory box!!

XXXII
Horse In The Sitting Room

Well, we advocates have been having training recently, and part of this training was looking at our Lone Working Policy, which provoked a deal of discussion. I like the discussions we have, it's great to hear different points of view to your own, and it broadens the mind-set ~ my mind not often "set", I can honestly say, but we advocates work on our own, and I love meeting up with the others to share our different experiences, of which there have been many.

Don't give up reading further at this point!! I know it sounds boring ~but stay with it if you can!

Going to clients' houses alone may be problematic, and so we have the option of meeting them at our office in Priory Street if possible, which is the preferred option. If not, then we venture forth into the unknown territory of clients' homes - (assessment having already been completed by a member of our office staff).

Sorry, I promised the boring bit would end ~ so here goes!

I was thinking of a time in my past life (THIS IS A TRUE STORY) when I lived in Catterick Garrison, and further along our road, lived a couple with a horse. Not very interesting so far then, but this horse lived in their house, with them!! I am assuming THEY actually slept in their bedroom, but the horse had his stable in their dining room, and the sitting room was a tack room where all the paraphernalia needed for horsey things was housed, including straw (or is it hay?). Never sure of country things, being a life-long townie! The "stable" had a patio door which opened onto the garden, where the horse had free reign over the greenery, and where the green very soon turned dark brown!!

Under the stairs where you and I may have housed the hoover, were the remains of earlier horsey meals ~ you know ~ the droppings that have to be cleared away, but were stashed there for all to see (and smell) if you chose to visit this peculiar trio.

I never did choose to visit, though I never knew the horse lived there. I would bump into the wife occasionally in the road ~ the sort of wife whose Barbour jacket and boots were the same colour as the pile of what-sit under the stairs!! And who always wore the mandatory silk Hermes scarf draped around her shoulders. She was always walking the horse, (she referred to it as THE HUNTER) just like others would walk a dog, and I really never gave her much thought, just the usual "morning" or "lovely day", and thought to myself that she was probably due to inherit a stately home, with a pile of dosh to go with it!!

Time went by, and it came time for us to move on. We were in Army quarters, as was the horse and his lookers-after, and we had to undergo the usual "march-out" where the house was inspected on our departure, and where the powers that be arrive with a torch to inspect the oven for any odd splash that may still be clinging for dear life to a shelf. Any mark found ANYWHERE has to be paid for at £1 per mark!! I am not joking!! In 29 years we never had to pay a penny. Not so for the horsey trio. They were charged tens of thousands of pounds ~ all floors replaced, plaster re-done all furniture replaced etc etc, and that is where I was correct in my earlier thinking!! They DID have money from a stately home, and they coughed up for the lot!! To them, I am sure, just the price to pay for keeping a horse.

So I should have known that our Lone Working Policy has to be taken seriously. Imagine the horror of walking into a client's home, and finding the above scenario, (or worse,) and, I feel for the members of staff who have to do an initial assessment!!! I am confident though ~ we have a great team in the office, and I am sure they would not bat an eye-lid, and would hopefully inform us to meet the client in the office!!

I have more tales to tell of "march-outs" from Army quarters if any of you are interested, and if you are ~ watch this space!!! And if you see anyone leading a horse down Priory Street, towards No 15 just let us know!! Please!!

XXXIII
Millennium New Year

Well, as usual in January we think to ourselves - "another New Year celebration came and went" - and I sincerely hope that this year is as good as you wish it to be for yourselves, your family and friends. One year it was lovely for myself and husband, as we spent it with old friends of over 30 years in their home in Chipping Sodbury. LOVELY!! She is the best cook we have ever known, she's Irish, and the best thing for her is to feed you till you cry for mercy!! What am I moaning about then, except to say we could hardly move from the table for hours at a time, her husband LOVES his wine, so the 2 of them together make the most delicious company, and we don't know what we would have done without them over the years. Happy New Year again to this lovely couple of friends.

Thinking back over past New Years, we seem to have spent it together with them either at our home or theirs for many of those 30 years, but not all. When we haven't, we have regretted it, ~ they though were probably grateful for the respite! The washing up is of truly epic proportions and the 4 of us stumble to bed in the early hours, usually still laughing.

We are older and more staid now ~ what have I said? Older yes, more staid is questionable.

I swear, the year I fell on their stairs, that only one glass of Prosecco had passed my lips, but the result on my back meant we had to leave early the next day to get home before it stiffened up too much to travel. Ouch. The promise of only one glass, no one believes, but it was true. It must have been the amount of food eaten!!

I am still harping back to celebrations with them, and thought to share our New Year's one at the new Millennium. They have stayed with us when we lived in Bristol, Harrogate, Ripon, Woolacombe in Devon, and in York. The Ripon occasion being the start of year 2000, the new Millennium, and so this particular one was an important one. Very Serious. After all, there were threats that planes would fall from the skies, computer systems everywhere would crash, and that our country would be plunged into darkness. So, having been warned of all these dire happenings, it was our plan for the morning of the New Day One of 2000 for the 4 of us to live in hope and trudge up the hill in Ripon, and to see the sun rise in a peaceful dawn in the hope that all would be well.

We prised ourselves from our beds at 6 am, all 4 having been out with our neighbours partying till 1 am - and with hats and scarves, and a bottle of Champagne with 4 glasses, off we set to see the New Year Dawn!!

Atop the hill, and with Ripon snuggled down below, we filled our glasses as the brightest orange dawn rose slowly in front of us. It was glorious! Breathtaking in fact, and as we looked at the Cathedral way down below us, the orange sun shone onto its windows, reflecting up across the sleeping houses in our direction so brightly it made us gasp.

I am not religious, but the sight was very moving to all 4 of us, and one I will never forget. No other light shining from

Ripon, except those reflected beams from the Cathedral windows. Happy New Year!!! And (for us) what a lovely way to start a new Millennium. Choked with emotion, and with empty tummies, we made our way back to our home, had some bacon rolls, and all fell asleep in front of a roaring fire. A truly treasured memory.

Happy New Year!

XXXIV
The End

Well, there you are, you survived the tedium of the snippets of my life, and who knows if you had a few laughs along the pages. I did as I was writing, and I hope it was the same for you ~ just know that you won't be thrown into the Tower if you didn't, I bear no grudges! Ok, then, I MIGHT, but will try harder next time ~ a scenario my old sports teacher would have approved of, and of course never happened! Not that I didn't want to try harder at sport ~ just never wanted to do it or watch it! Ever! (BBC, please take note~how dare you!)

Always one to end with a smile, I will pass this remark from one of my grandsons. At age 11, he had been prone to attract the opposite sex since he was about 6, and at 7 came out with the very funny line, "I think it's best if I stay 'Single' in Primary!" Oh dear, I see trouble ahead!

Thank you for reading, from a very grateful Lighthouse.